Hi, everyone! It's your favorite friend and captain, Frankie! Floyd and I are going on a trip to Island today. Join us for a fantastic adven

See these coins? Every time you learn something new, you get one of these stickers to put in your money sack. When you finish each section, you'll get a treasure sticker to put on your Certificate of Completion at the end of the book.

See this picture of me? When you see this picture on the page, it means I'm there to give you a little help. Just look for **Frankie's Facts**.

Are you ready? Raise the sails, we're off!

Frankie's Facts

There are 21 **consonants** in the alphabet. A consonant is any letter that is not a vowel.

Ahoy! We're sailing to Tree Fort Island. Can you help us get there? **Say the picture name on each ship. Circle the consonant that stands for the beginning sound.**

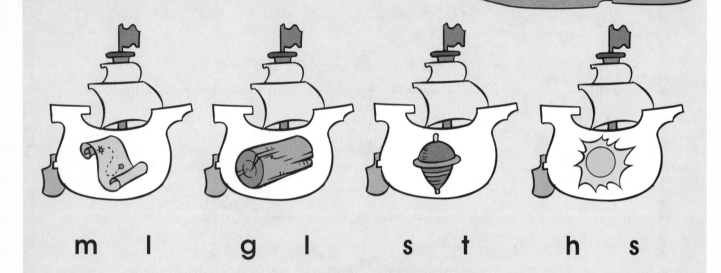

m l   g l   s t   h s

We're almost there! Now circle the consonant that stands for the ending sound in each picture name below.

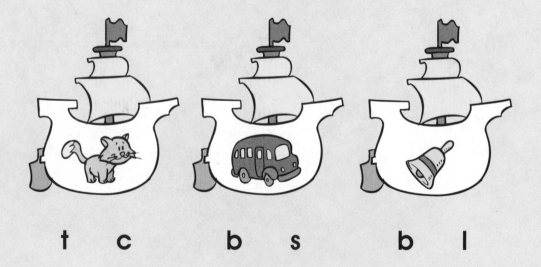

t c   b s   b l

Let's play in the leaves around the tree fort! **Say the picture name in each leaf. Write the missing beginning or ending consonant on the line.**

___ose   fro___   ___ite

fo___   ___ate

bea___   soc___

Help me find some acorns for a tree fort snack!

Say the picture name in each acorn. Write the missing beginning or ending letter on the line.

__ ----

__oat

__ ----

__all

__ ----

cra__

__ ----

be__

__ ----

__orm

__ ----

__esk

__ ----

__an

__ ----

tu__

Look at the ladders to the tree fort! Help us climb up.

Circle the picture whose name has the beginning or ending consonant shown at the bottom of the ladder. Then write the letters on the lines to finish the words.

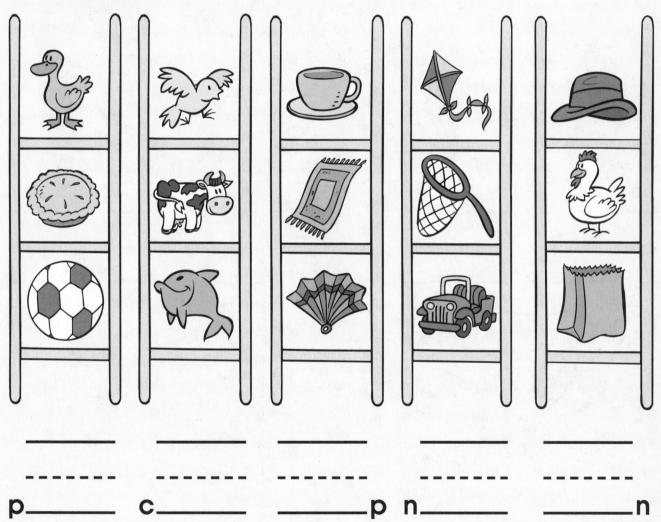

p_____   c_____   _____p   n_____   _____n

It's fun to watch the squirrels run through the tree branches! They want to squirrel some things away inside the tree.
Say each picture name. Write the consonants that stand for the beginning and ending sounds of each.

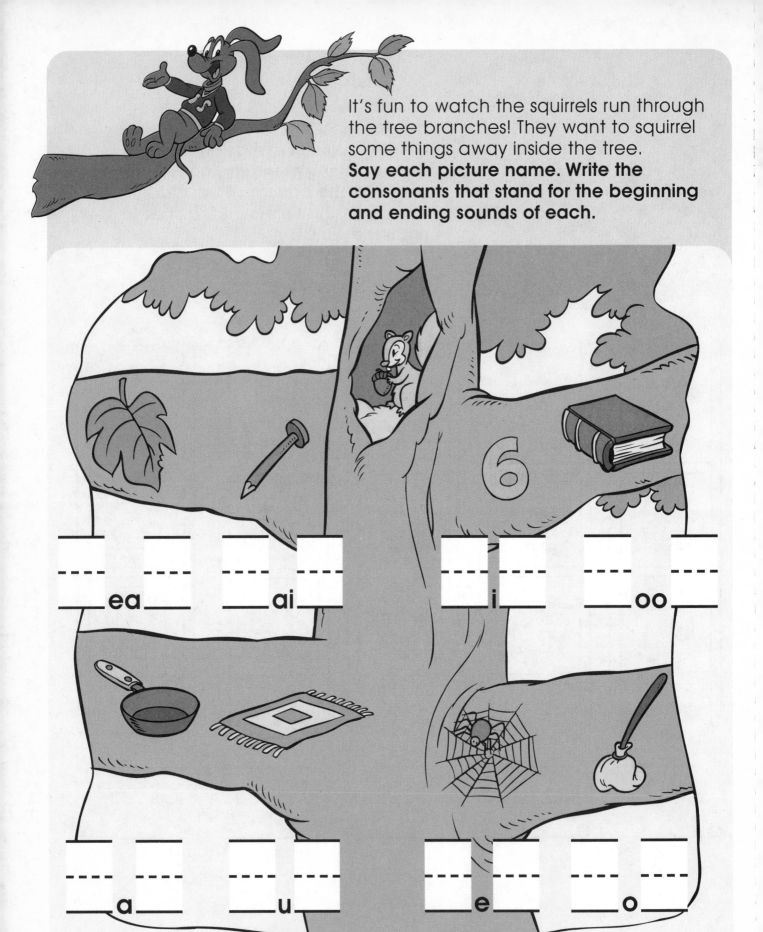

____ ea ____   ____ ai ____   ____ i ____   ____ oo ____

____ a ____   ____ u ____   ____ e ____   ____ o ____

It's lunchtime! Let's fill our bowls. Look at the letter on each bowl. Draw a line to the picture word it completes. Then write the letter on the line.

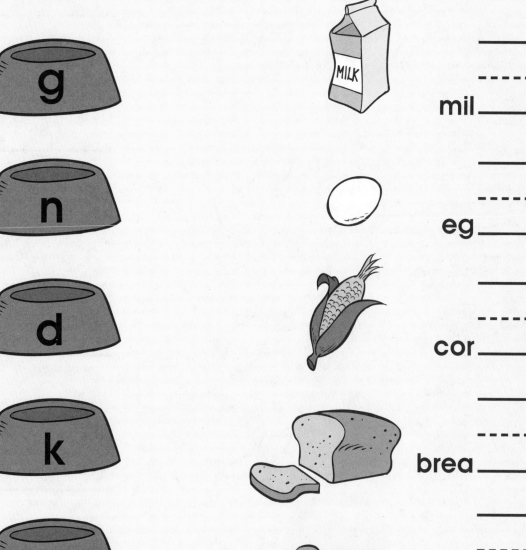

mil _____

eg _____

cor _____

brea _____

nu _____

Great! Put your coin sticker in your money sack and jump ahead.

Consonants 7

I'm watching birds. You can, too! Help each bird find its nest. **Say the name of the picture in each nest. Then find a bird that matches the beginning sound. Draw a line to connect them. Then write the word on the line. Circle the consonant that makes the beginning sound.**

I've created a secret code for us to use on Tree Fort Island!
Draw a line from the pictures to the correct words. Then write the letter that starts each word.

 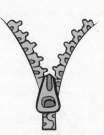  

___ ___ ___ ___

___ipper   ___o-yo   ___eep   ___ase

Now use the code to crack the secret message! Look at the letter next to each beginning consonant in the secret code box. Each consonant you wrote has a secret letter match. Write the matching letters in order on the lines below.

___ ___ ___

___ ___ ___ ___

___ ___ ___ ___

SECRET CODE
z = b
y = a
j = r
v = k

What do dogs and trees have in common?

_____

We both have a _____!

Excellent job! Put your coin sticker in your money sack and jump ahead.

Consonants　9

What can you see inside the tree fort?
Look at the words in the word box. Put an X on every word you can find in the picture. Then sort them all by their beginning consonants.

bird	juice	milk	leaf	bed	pan
book	zoo	pail	fox	flag	bus
yo-yo	light	mask	door	bear	
drum	fan	pillow	map	fork	

Words that begin with **m** or **l**

_____map_____

_____leaf_____

_____

_____

Words that begin with **b** or **d**

_____

_____

_____

_____

_____

Words that begin with **p** or **f**

_____

_____

_____

_____

_____

Words that begin with **j**, **z**, or **y**

_____

_____

_____

Nice job! Place your goblet sticker on your Certificate of Completion and jump ahead.

Review 11

Frankie's Facts

The letters **a**, **e**, **i**, **o**, and **u** are **vowels**. Vowels between two consonants usually make a **short** sound. The short vowel sounds are **a** as in c**a**t, **e** as in n**e**t, **i** as in f**i**sh, **o** as in b**o**x, and **u** as in r**u**g.

I am making special tree fort hats.
**Say the picture name on each hat.
Circle the letter that stands for its short
vowel sound.**

Whee! Swinging from the tree fort is fun!

Say the vowel name under each pair of pictures. Circle the picture in each pair with that vowel sound.

short e

short a

short i

short o

short u

Way to go! Put your coin sticker in your money sack and jump ahead.

We're hungry again! Help us get to the snacks. **Say each picture name. Write a vowel to finish each word.**

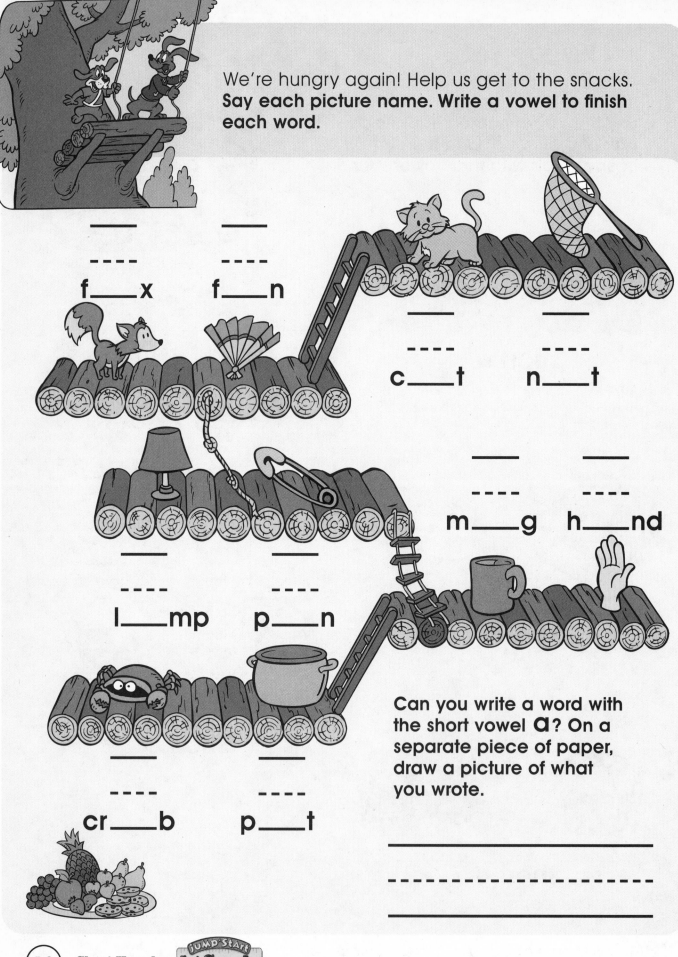

f__x   f__n

c__t   n__t

m__g   h__nd

l__mp   p__n

cr__b   p__t

Can you write a word with the short vowel **a**? On a separate piece of paper, draw a picture of what you wrote.

_____

- - - - - - - - - - - - - - - - - -

_____

I'm watching some birds hatch.
You can watch, too!
**Say the picture name on each egg.
Then fill in the short vowels to finish
each word.**

1. s___ck

2. h___t

3. b___g

4. r___ck

5. fr___g

6. b___t

7. h___n

8. f___x

9. l___ck

10. l___ps

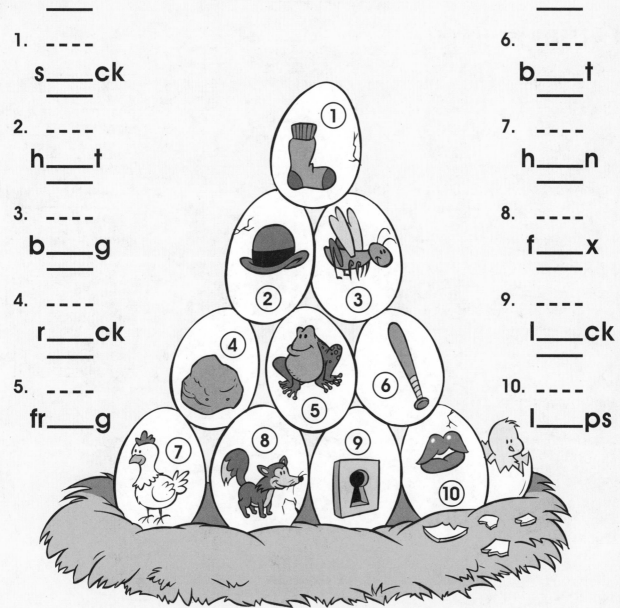

**Can you write a word with the short vowel O?
On a separate piece of paper, draw a picture
of what you wrote.**

_____

- - - - - - - - - - - - - -

_____

Floyd is cleaning the tree fort. Can you help him put some things away?

Write the vowel i to complete each word. Then draw a line to the matching picture.

sh___p

p___g

ch___ck

g___ft

f___sh

Can you write a word with the short vowel i?
On a separate piece of paper, draw a picture
of what you wrote.

_____

- - - - - - - - - - - -

_____

Floyd is climbing trees. You can, too!
Say the name of each picture. Write the missing vowel to complete that word. Then write the words with short vowel **u** and short vowel **e** in the box.

b____s

dr____m

sl____d

p____n

b____ll

b____g

short u	short e
_____	_____
_____	_____
_____	_____

Terrific climbing! Put your coin sticker in your money sack and jump ahead.

Will you help me fix up the tree fort? Say each picture name and write the missing vowel. One picture name on each table has a short vowel. Circle it.

m___t

r___ke

b___ne

c___p

b___ll

k___te

Acorns are falling on me! Help!
Circle and write the word that names the picture. Then put an X on the word if it makes a short vowel sound.

pine   pin

_ _ _ _ _ _ _ _ _ _ _ _

pan   pane

_ _ _ _ _ _ _ _ _ _ _ _

bead   bed

_ _ _ _ _ _ _ _ _ _ _ _

bone   coat

_ _ _ _ _ _ _ _ _ _ _ _

cat   cake

_ _ _ _ _ _ _ _ _ _ _ _

You did it! Put your coin sticker in your money sack and jump ahead.

Short Vowels 19

Level 3

Come on! Let's go on a short vowel nature walk!
Follow the arrows along the path. Say each picture name. Write the missing vowel to finish each word. Keep going until you reach the lake!

START

___gg

fr___g

f___x

s___n

r___ck

d___ck

c__t

b__t

n___st

st___ck

m__p

FINISH

Stupendous! Place your scepter sticker on
your Certificate of Completion and jump ahead.

Review 21

Frankie's Facts

Long vowels say their name. The long vowel sounds are **a** as in c**a**ke, **e** as in f**ee**t, **o** as in r**o**pe, **i** as in d**i**me, and **u** as in c**u**te.

We're swinging on a tire swing! **Say each picture name. Then add long vowels to complete each word.**

___ce

c___ke

f___ ___t

r___se

g___te

b___ ___

k___te

c___ne

Help us keep swinging!
Draw a line from each picture to the tire with the same vowel sound.

long a

long e

long o

long u

**Super job! Put your coin sticker in
your money sack and jump ahead.**

Frankie's Facts

Sometimes the letter **e** is silent in words that have a long vowel sound, like c**a**p**e**.

Let's see what we find when we look through my binoculars.
Write the missing letters to finish the long a words I see.

_ _ _ _
_ _ _ a _ es

_ _ _
_ a _ e

_ _ _ _
_ _ a _ e

_ _ _ _
_ a _ e

_ _ _
_ _ a _ e

Can you write another word that has the long a sound?

_ _ _ _ _ _ _ _ _ _ _ _ _

Help me make silent **e** masks in the tree fort!
Circle the word that names the picture. Then write the word on the line.

mile
smile
mill

_____
- - - - - - - - - - - - - - -
_____

prize
pies
rise

_____
- - - - - - - - - - - - - - -
_____

slid
lid
slide

_____
- - - - - - - - - - - - - - -
_____

five
have
hive

_____
- - - - - - - - - - - - - - -
_____

kite
kit
tie

_____
- - - - - - - - - - - - - - -
_____

dim
dime
dome

_____
- - - - - - - - - - - - - - -
_____

Can you write another word that has the long **i** sound? _____
- -

Come and watch the stars with us!
Read the words in the box. Then look at the pictures in the stars. Pick the word that goes in each sentence and write it on the line.

bone	stove	stone	hose

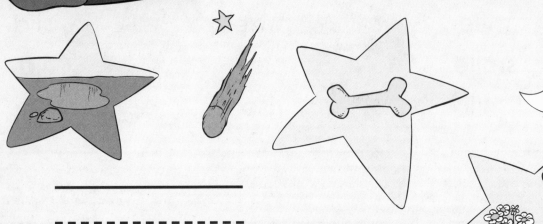

The _____ is by the lake.

The _____ is for a dog.

You can get water from a _____.

Dad cooks dinner on a _____.

Can you write another word that has the long **O** sound?

Look at all the cloud shapes!
Say the picture name in each cloud. Color in the clouds with pictures whose names have a long U sound. Then write the vowels to finish each word.

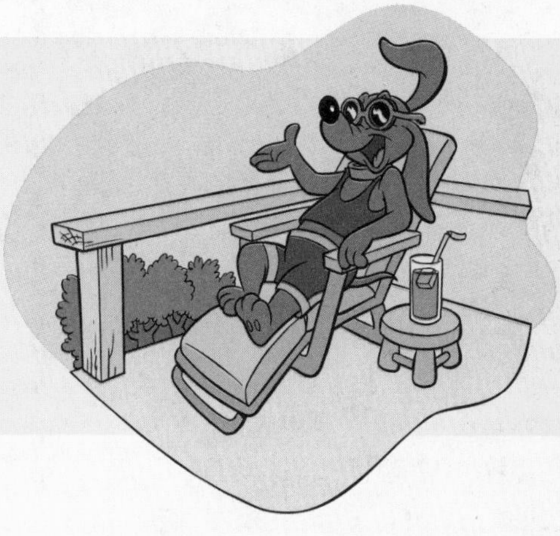

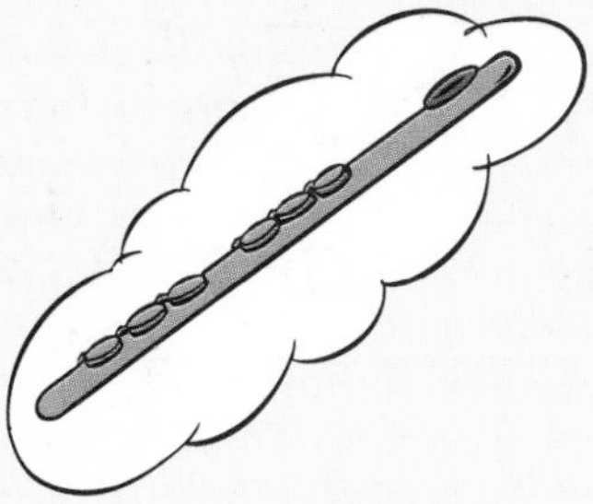

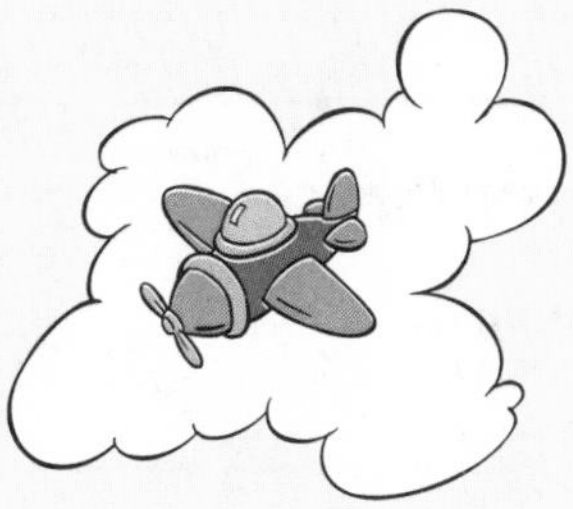

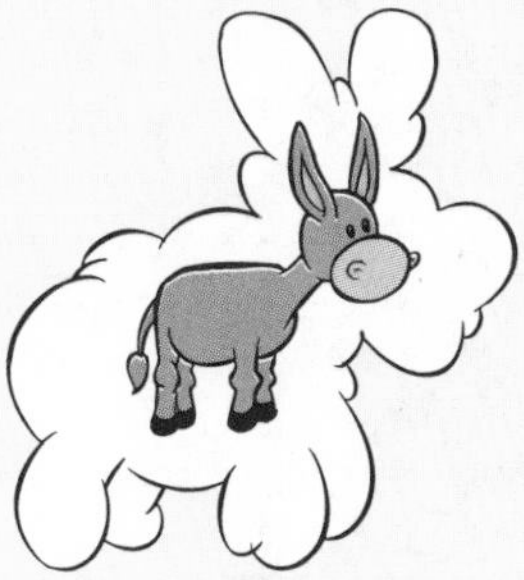

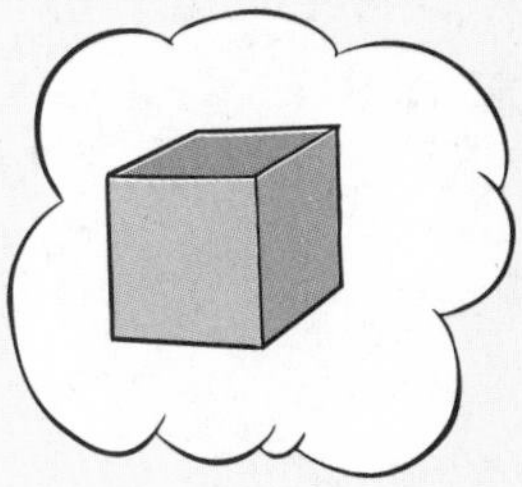

fl___t___ pl___n___ m___l___ c___b___

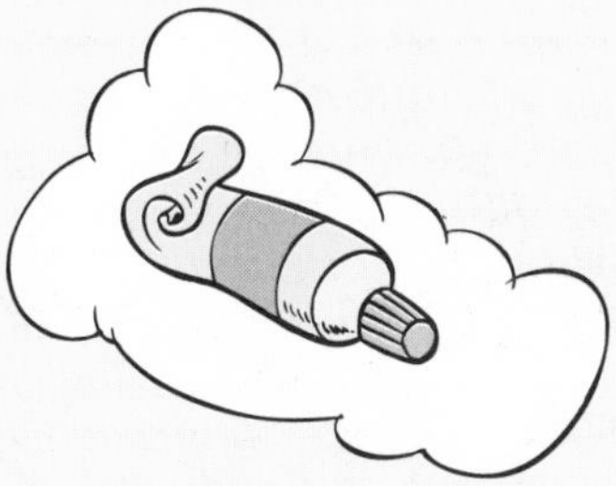

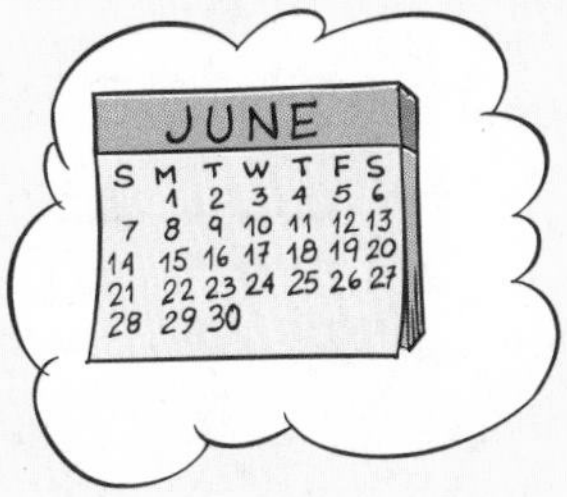

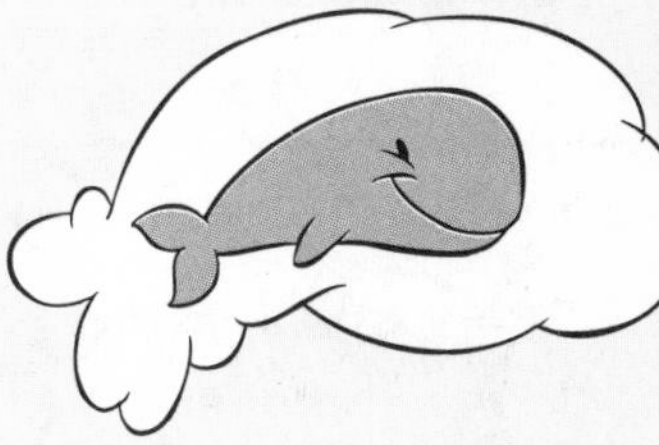

f___v___ t___b___ J___n___ wh___l___

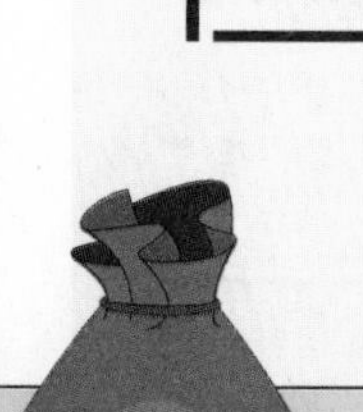

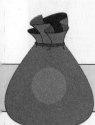

Fantastic! Put your coin sticker in your money sack and jump ahead.

Frankie's Facts

Vowels that have a **consonant** after them are usually short. Vowels that are followed by a **consonant** and a **silent e** usually make a long sound.

cap   cape

We're at the Tree Fort Island beach! **Say the name of each picture and write that word on the line. If the word has a short vowel, color the shell red. If the word has a long vowel, color the shell blue.**

globe	lamp	bone
frog	skates	cake

_____

- - - - - - - - - - -

_____

- - - - - - - - - - -

_____

- - - - - - - - - - -

_____

- - - - - - - - - - -

_____

- - - - - - - - - - -

_____

- - - - - - - - - - -

Help Floyd plant flowers!
Use these letters to make words with long vowel sounds.

h   k   e

___
- - - -
___ole

___
- - - -
cut___

___
- - - -
ma___e

___
- - - -
___ite

How many words can you think of that rhyme with the word "gate"?

Excellent job! Put your coin sticker in your money sack and jump ahead.

Long Vowels   **29**

Frankie and I are having a party in the tree fort. You're invited, of course!

Read each word in the box and circle the picture at the party. Only two of these words have a short vowel. Circle those two words in the word box.

Now, let's play a party game!
Find the words from the word box in this puzzle. Circle them all.

cake
game
kite
rose
rug
drink
cheese
plate
vase

p l a t e c
c b d c d h
a e r o s e
k k i t e e
e f n v g s
h i k a a e
r u g s m i
m p s e e u

Congratulations! You did it! Place your crown sticker on your Certificate of Completion.

Answer Key

PAGE 2   circle m, l, t, s; t, s, l

PAGE 3   write r, g, k, x, g, r, k

PAGE 4   write c, b, b, d, w, d, c, b

PAGE 5   circle pie, cow, cup, net, hen; write ie, ow, cu, et, he

PAGE 6   write l/f, n/l, s/x, b/k, p/n, r/g, w/b, m/p

PAGE 7   draw lines to connect g/egg, n/corn, d/bread, k/milk, t/nut; write k, g, n, d, t

PAGE 8   draw lines to connect vest/v, juice/j, jam/j, zebra/z, van/v; write zebra, vest or van, van or vest, jam or juice, juice or jam; circle z, v, v, j, j

PAGE 9   draw lines to connect jeep/ eep, zipper/ipper, yo-yo/ o-yo, vase/ase; write z, y, j, v; write b, a, r, k; write bark

PAGES 10–11   write X on all words in word box; for m or l words write light, milk, mask; for p or f words write fan, pail, pillow, fox, flag, fork, pan; for b or d words write bird, book, drum, door, bed, bear, bus; for j, z, or y words write yo-yo, juice, zoo

PAGE 12   circle e, o, a, u, i

PAGE 13   circle tent, hat, pig, clock, mug

PAGE 14   write o, a; a, e; u, a; a, i; a, o; answers will vary

PAGE 15   write o, a, u, o, o, a, e, o, o, i; answers will vary

PAGE 16   write i five times; answers will vary

PAGE 17   write (from top) u, u, e, e, e, u; for short u words write drum, bus, bug; for short e words write pen, sled, bell

PAGE 18   write a, a, o, u, e, i; circle mat, cup, bell

PAGE 19   circle and write pin, pan, bed, coat, cake; draw an X on pin, pan, bed

PAGES 20–21   write e, o, u, a, a, e, i, o, u, o, a

PAGE 22   write i, a, ee, o, a, ee, i, o

PAGE 23   draw lines to connect rope/long o, rake/long a, feet/long e, mule/long u

PAGE 24   write sk/t, r/k, pl/n, pl/t, sn/k; answers will vary

PAGE 25   circle and write smile, prize, slide, hive, kite, dime; answers will vary

PAGE 26   write stone, bone, hose, stove; answers will vary

PAGE 27   color clouds with mule, cube; write u/e, a/e, u/e, u/e, i/e, u/e, u/e, a/e

PAGE 28   write lamp, frog, cake, skates, globe, bone; color shells red with lamp and frog; color shells blue with cake, skates, globe, bone

PAGE 29   write h, e, k, k; answers will vary

PAGES 30–31   circle cake, game, kite, rose, rug, drink, cheese, plate, vase in picture; circle the words rug, drink

Hi! I'm Frankie, a top dog around this school. This is my pal Floyd. He's the hall monitor. Why don't you come into school with us? We'll find all sorts of treasures. You'll feel right at home in no time.

See these coins? Each time you learn something new, you get one of these stickers to put in your money sack. When you finish a whole section, you'll get a big treasure sticker to put on your Certificate of Completion at the end of the book.

One more thing! Check out this picture of me. That's my way of helping you! Just look for **Frankie's Facts**.

So let's hurry! I just heard the school bell ring.

Frankie's Facts

A **beginning sound** is the sound the first letter in a word makes.

dog

Oops! The school door is shut. You'll need to ring all the bells to open it. **Say the name of the picture on each bell. Then find the letter that stands for its beginning sound. Draw a line from that button to the bell.**

Welcome to JumpStart school! Floyd has a hall pass ready for you.

To use it, just match the picture on each door to its beginning sound. Say the picture name. Then color in the space with the correct letter.

p	d	l
t	s	f

l	m	d
s	p	i

t	l	s
m	p	d

d	p	t
s	m	l

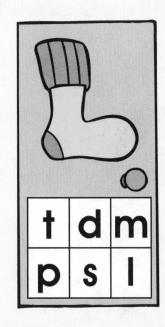

t	d	m
p	s	l

p	s	i
t	d	m

Way to go! Put your coin sticker in your money sack and jump ahead to the next level.

What great pictures the students have made!
Say each picture name. Then write the letter that makes its
beginning sound. Look on the board for clues.

On a separate
piece of paper,
draw your own
picture. What is
it? Write the
letter it starts
with here:

_____

_ _ _ _ _ _ _ _ _ _

_____

What a mess! Help me clean up all these blocks.
**Say each picture name and listen to its beginning sound.
Then write down its first letter. Look at the blocks for clues.**

____ose

____en

____ut

____ing

____an

____us

____ig

____ar

Frankie's Facts

Some letters look alike. Look at each one carefully:

w   m   p   d

Ms. Nobel, our teacher, loves to make signs for the things in the classroom. She left the first letters for you to fill in.
Choose the correct letters from the table and write them on the lines.

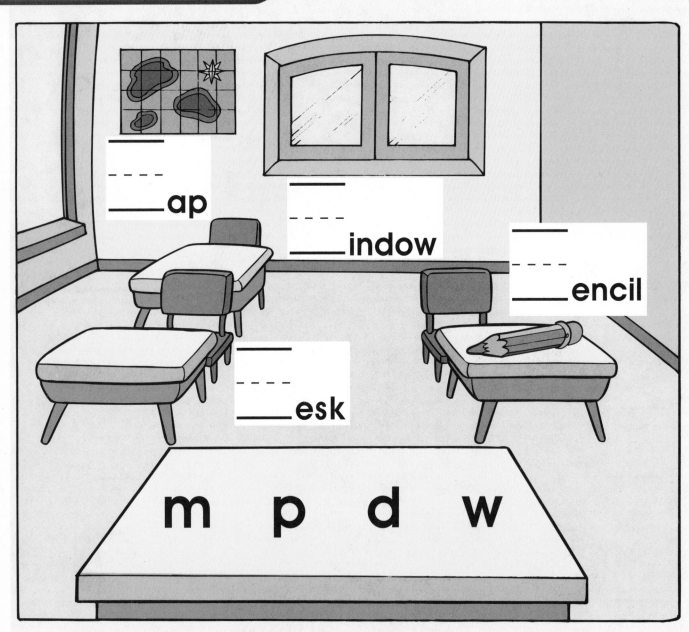

____ap

____indow

____encil

____esk

m   p   d   w

Can you think of something else to write with that begins with p? (Hint: It's part of the word "pencil.")

There are Frisbees on the playground! Let's play a game with them.

Look at the pictures on the pairs of Frisbees. Say each picture name. If the two picture names start with the same sound, write the letter for that sound on the line. If they don't, leave the line blank.

_____   _____

- - - - - -   - - - - - -

_____   _____

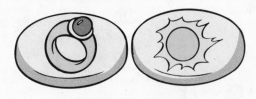    

_____   _____

- - - - - -   - - - - - -

_____   _____

_____   _____

- - - - - -   - - - - - -

_____   _____

_____   _____

- - - - - -   - - - - - -

_____   _____

Great job! Put your coin sticker in your money sack and jump ahead to the next level!

Beginning Sounds   39

Level 2

Frankie's Facts

Some letters have the same sound. The beginning sound of "c" in **cat** sounds like the beginning sound of "k" in **kite**.

Look what floated in the open window!
Can you match the letters in the box to the beginning sound of each picture name? Write the letter on the line. Then color in the balloons.

j z k v

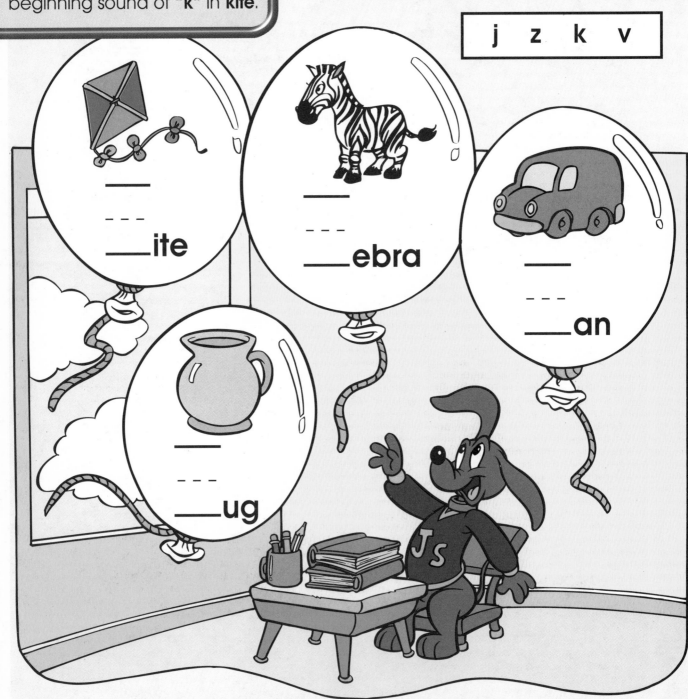

___ite

___ebra

___an

___ug

Do you like puzzles? Try these.
Look at the pictures next to each puzzle. Their picture names start with the same letter. Choose the correct letter from Frankie's cards to finish them. Write it in the box.

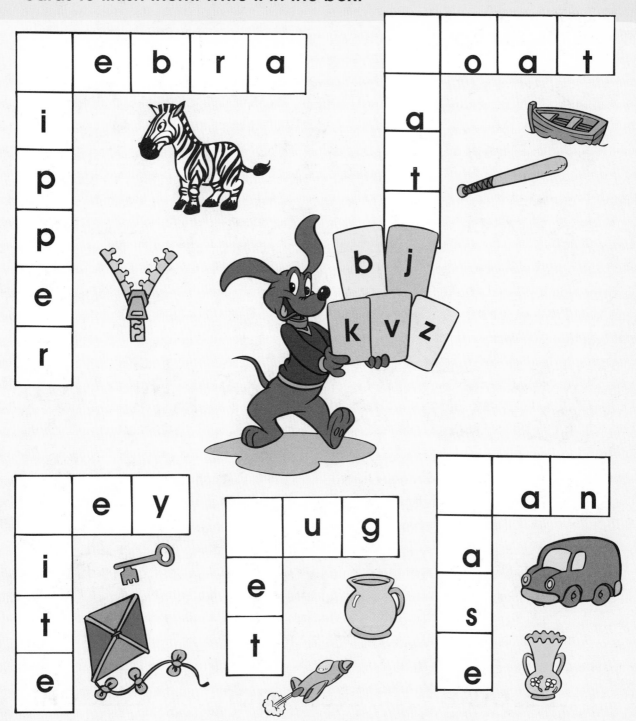

Now look at the van/vase puzzle. Which other letters could you put in the square to make two new words?

You've solved the puzzles! Put your coin sticker in your money sack and jump ahead!

There's time to play a beanbag game before lunch.

duck

____ eaf

____ un

m   l   s   t   d   w

____ ouse

____ agon

____ ent

Look at the letters on each beanbag. Throw the letters into the correct spot by matching them to the picture with that beginning sound. Write the letters on the lines.

_____an   _____at   _____all

_____est   _____ox   _____ake

Frankie's Facts

An **ending sound** is the sound the last letter in a word makes.

Pin ends with the sound **"n."**

It's lunchtime. You can sit with Floyd and me. The letters on these lunch boxes have the same ending sound as the things on our table.
Say each picture name out loud. Then draw a line from each letter to the thing with the same ending sound.

Help us line up for class.
Look at the first row and say the picture names on our T-shirts. Draw a line to match the ending sounds in the first row to the beginning sounds in the second row. The letters below us will help you match the pictures.

t   d   g   n

d   n   t   g

Well done! Put your coin sticker in your money sack and jump ahead.

I'm all ears for music class. How about you?
Say the picture name on each music stand.
Write the letter that stands for the ending sound
on the line. Then draw lines to match the letters
you wrote to the letters on the music pages.

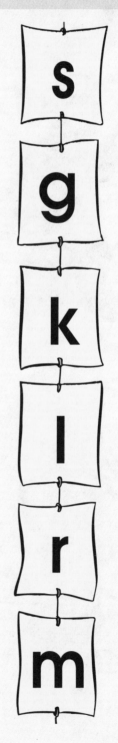

Help us sound out the words that are coming from our instruments.
**Say each picture name out loud. Then write the ending sound of
each picture name on the line. Choose from the letters in the box.**

**Can you think of something that ends with an L? Say its name.
(Hint: There are usually four of them in every room!)**

Do you like computer games? Play this one with me.
Say the name of each picture. On the line under it, write the keyboard letter that matches its ending sound. Then color in that key on the keyboard.

Write the letters from the keyboard that you did not use. Can you think of words that end with these letters?

We made mobiles of animal pictures. Now let's add their names. **Say each picture name and listen for its ending sound. Then look for that letter in the box and write it on the line.**

b l m p n g

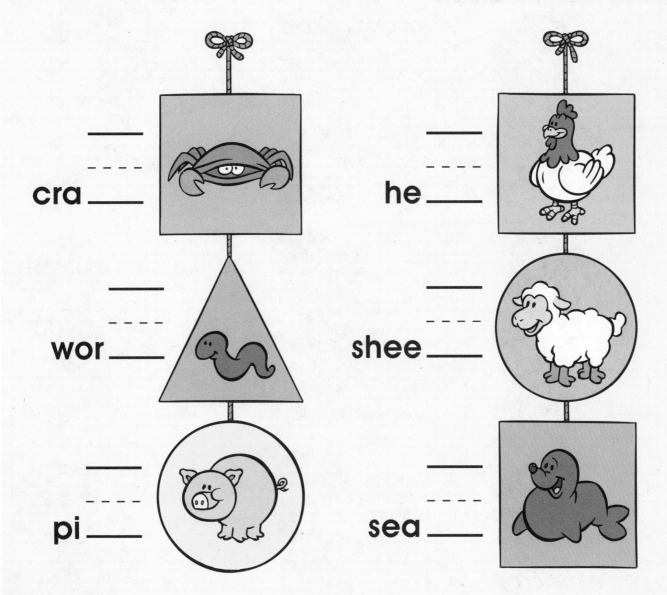

cra ____

wor ____

pi ____

he ____

shee ____

sea ____

Frankie's Facts

Some ending sounds are similar. You have to listen carefully to tell them apart. The letters **N** and **M** sound alike.

Play ball! We need four kids for the **N** team and four kids for the **M** team. **Say the picture name on each T-shirt out loud. If it ends with the "n" sound, write an N on the line. If it ends with the "m" sound, write an M on the line.**

How about a game between the **P** team and the **T** team?
Write the last letter of each picture name on the lines. Then count how many of each letter you have. The team with the most ending sounds wins!

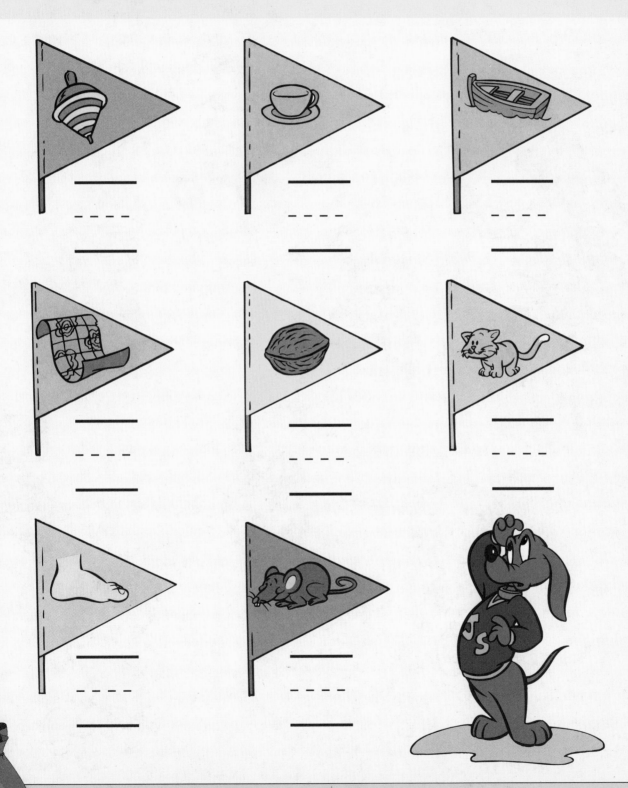

You're a winner, too! Put your coin sticker in your money sack and jump ahead!

Ending Sounds 51

Level 3

We're playing musical chairs with letters! There are 9 players but only 8 chairs. Stop the music!

Draw a line from each letter to the chair with the picture name that ends in the same sound. Start with me, Frankie. Which child does not get a chair? Circle that player.

You rule the class. Put your throne sticker on your Certificate of Completion and jump ahead.

Review 53

Frankie's Facts

The middle sound in a word is often a **vowel**: **a, e, i, o,** or **u**. In the word **cat**, it is the **short a** sound.

cat   web   mitt   top   hut

It's pet day in school! Look at all the cats! What is each one playing with? **Say the picture name aloud and listen for the middle sound. If it is a short a, color the cat brown. If it is not a short a, color the cat orange.**

The spider is the teacher's favorite animal. Look at the pictures around the spider's web.
Find the three picture names with the middle sound of short e, as in web. Draw a line from the spider to each one.

Way to go! Put your coin sticker in your money sack and jump ahead to the next level!

Frankie's Facts

Vowels can also have **long** sounds. The middle sound in **rake** is **long a**. In **bike** it is **long i**. In **bone** it is **long o**.

rake   bike   bone

Help us choose our library books! We can each pick one.
Look at the picture on each T-shirt. Say the picture name aloud. Then find the book that has the same middle sound as the T-shirt. Color them both the same color.

Frankie's Facts

The middle sound of **long e** is often spelled **ee**, as in **seed**, or **ea**, as in **bean**.

feet   beans

Look at the words next to each body part. Three of them have the middle sound of **long e**, as in **seed**. **Circle them.**

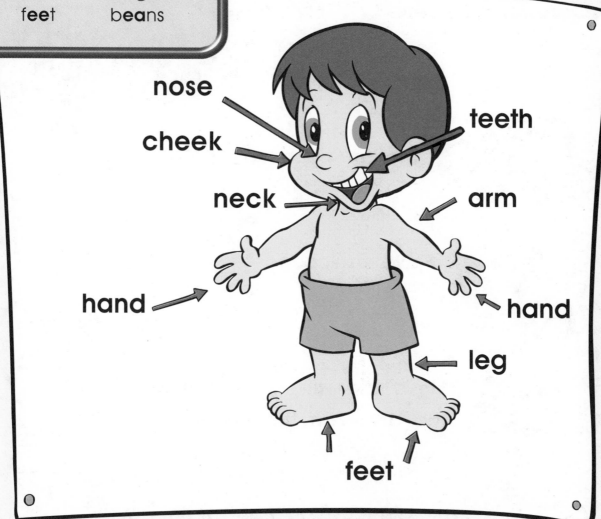

nose

cheek

teeth

neck

arm

hand

hand

leg

feet

Now circle the word that has the same middle sound as cube.

bug   mule   sun

Frankie's Facts

An **e** at the end of a word is silent. It usually makes the vowel sound before it long. The **a** in **rake** is a **long a**.

Can you crack the secret code? The pictures give you clues. **Use the code to figure out which long vowels belong in each sentence. Then write the correct one on the line.**

a ee i o u

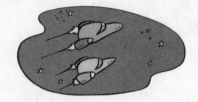
The n◯me of the g◯me is "Sp◯ce R◯ce."

_____

F◯ve m◯ce go for a b◯ke r◯de.

_____

Floyd uses his n◯se to find the b◯ne in the h◯le.

_____

The c◯te m◯le has h◯ge ears.

_____

The gr◯n sh◯p has red f◯t.

_____

The kids in class have made a game for you.
Fill in one long vowel in each puzzle. Look closely at the kids for picture clues.

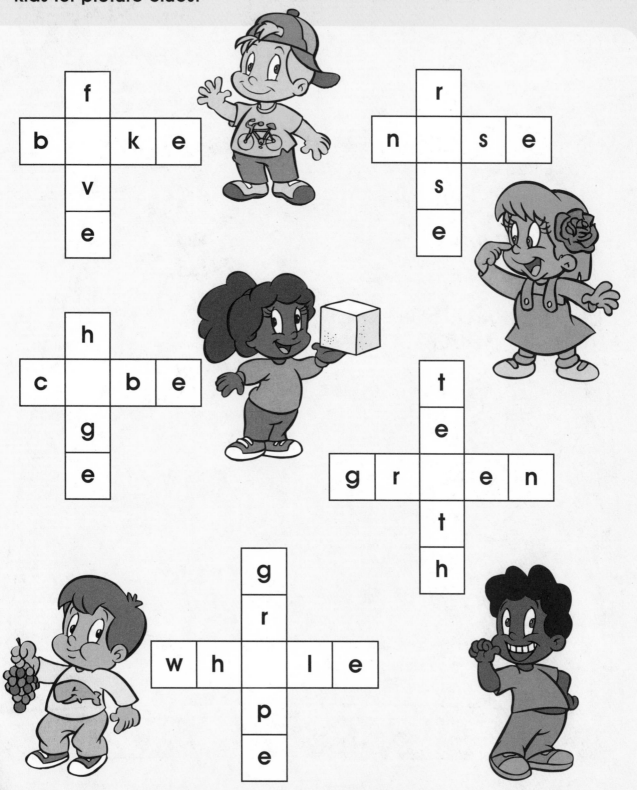

Bow-WOW. You did it! Put your coin sticker in your money sack and jump ahead to the next level!

Look what we found in the sandbox!
Say each picture name. Then draw a line to match the ones with the same middle sound.

What a funny group of things on the playground! You can match them by their middle sounds.

Say each picture name. Fill in the missing vowel. Then draw a line between the pictures with the same middle long vowel sound.

sl___de

sw___ng

m___le

k___te

b___e

b___ne

r___pe

c___be

You did it! Put your coin sticker in your money sack and jump ahead!

Middle Sounds 61

School is out! It's time to hop aboard our ship and sail for home.
Walk with me! The path is full of pictures for you to name.
Fill in the missing letters as you go. Then color the squares with long vowels green and the squares with short vowels red.

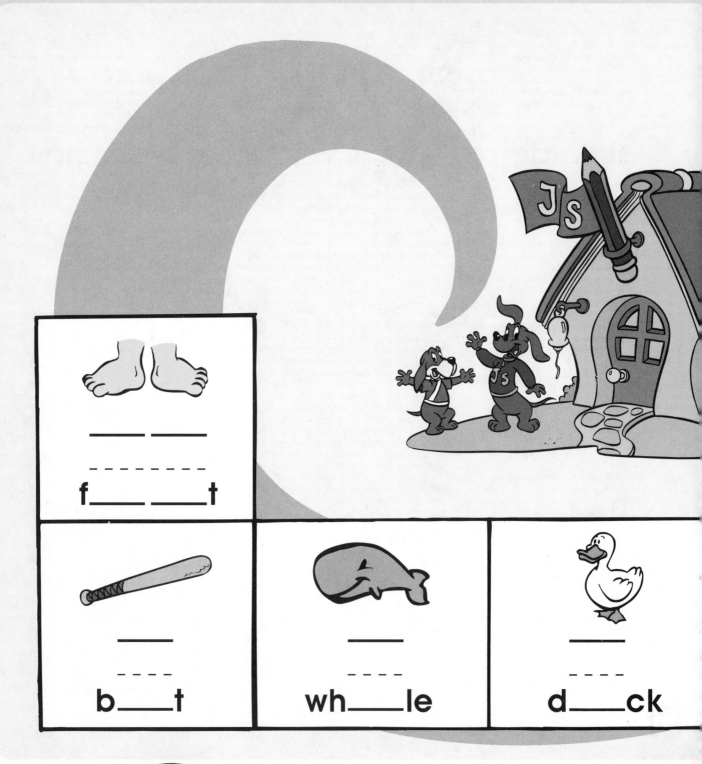

f____ ____t

b____t

wh____le

d____ck

c___be

n___st

b___ke

cl___ck

r___pe

c___ke

You walk with the best! Place your gem
sticker on your Certificate of Completion.

Review 63

Answer Key

PAGE 34	draw lines to connect d/dog, m/moon, p/pot, l/lock, s/sun, t/top
PAGE 35	color in spaces d, l, m, p, s, t
PAGE 36	write h, b, n, r, w, f, c, o; answers will vary
PAGE 37	write (left column) n, h, n, r; (right column) f, b, w, c
PAGE 38	write m for map, w for window, p for pencil, d for desk; pen
PAGE 39	write c for carrot/cake, p for pig/pie, t for top/tire, h for hat/heart
PAGE 40	write k for kite, z for zebra, v for van, j for jug
PAGE 41	write z for zebra/zipper, b for boat/bat, k for key/kite, j for jug/jet, v for van/vase; answers will vary
PAGE 42	match and write l, s, m, w, t
PAGE 43	match and write c, h, b, n, f, r
PAGE 44	draw lines to connect p/cup, b/bib, t/carrot, n/spoon
PAGE 45	draw lines to connect bird/dog, pig/goat, sun/nest
PAGE 46	connect and write m, l, g, s, r, k
PAGE 47	write d, g, k, m, r, s
PAGE 48	write k, l, r, m, s, t; color in k, l, r, m, s, t on keyboard; write unused letters b, p, d, g
PAGE 49	write (left column) b, m, g; (right column) n, p, l
PAGE 50	write M, M, N, N, N, M, M, N
PAGE 51	write P, P, T, P, T, T, T
PAGES 52–53	draw lines to connect d/bed, g/pig, s/bus, n/pan, t/rat, l/wheel, m/jam, r/car; circle b
PAGE 54	color brown cat with bat, cat with mat, cat with bag; color remaining cats orange
PAGE 55	draw lines to connect spider to nest, hen, bed
PAGE 56	color train/cake, boat/rope, bike/mice
PAGE 57	circle cheek, teeth, feet; circle mule
PAGE 58	write a, i, o, u, ee
PAGE 59	write i, o, u, e, a
PAGE 60	draw lines to connect lock/pot, hen/pen, shell/bell, bag/hat
PAGE 61	write (left column) i, u, e, o; (right column) i, i, o, u; draw lines to connect slide/kite, mule/cube, bee/swing, rope/bone
PAGES 62–63	write ee, a, a, u, o, a, o, i, u, e; color green feet, whale, rope, cake, bike, cube; color red bat, duck, clock, nest

Ahoy! It's Captain Frankie here. Floyd and I are on the way to our ship. We're sailing to Toy Island today. Come join our crew! Fun lies ahead!

See these coins? Every time you finish learning something new, you get one of these stickers to put in your money sack. When you finish each section, you'll get a treasure to put on your Certificate of Completion at the end of the book.

See this picture of me? When you see this picture on the page, it means I'm there to give you a little help. Just look for **Frankie's Facts.**

I feel a strong breeze. Let's hurry! It's a great day for sailing!

Frankie's Facts

Words with the same middle and ending sounds **rhyme**. M<u>op</u> and t<u>op</u> are rhyming words.

Floyd is cleaning up before we sail. **Help him match things that rhyme. Say each picture name. Then draw a line between the pictures with the same middle and ending sounds.**

Can you think of something else that rhymes with hat? Draw it here.

A good captain always checks the weather before sailing. Can you help me figure out this weather report?
Look at the rebus pictures below. Say them out loud! Now fill in the missing letters to complete each word.

Today will be **fun**.
There should be lots of _____

_____ **un.**

If the sun shines a **lot**,
it will get very _____

_____ **ot.**

It would be a good **plan**
to take along a _____

_____ **an.**

This news is the **best**.
Winds will come from the  _____

_____ **est.**

Sailing is a **snap**
when you have a good _____

_____ **ap.**

Way to go! Put your coin sticker on your money sack and jump ahead.

Rhymes and Phonograms **67**

Frankie's Facts

Certain sounds and letters can work together, just like a family. Dog and frog belong to the og **word family**, or **phonogram**.

Full speed ahead to Toy Island! Let's fill the sails! **Say the two picture names on each sail. Write in these endings to finish the rhyming words.**

-at -an -og -ock

On a separate piece of paper, draw a picture of something with a name that rhymes with sail.

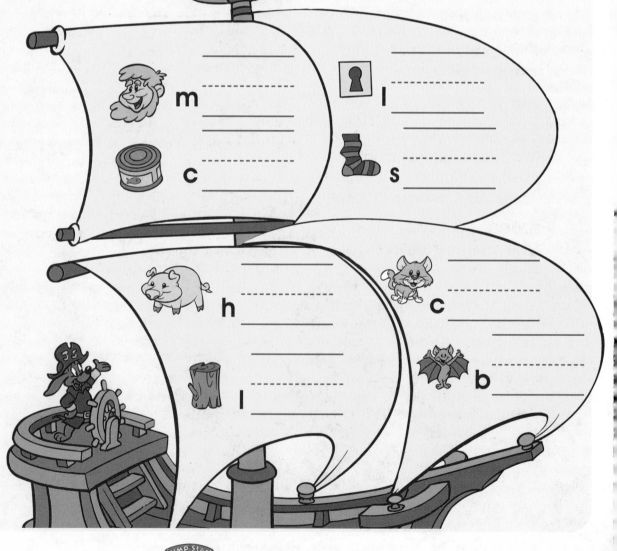

m _____

c _____

l _____

s _____

h _____

l _____

c _____

b _____

Let's go fishing for rhyming words. **Find the fish with picture names that rhyme. Draw a line between each rhyming pair.**

pig

king

bib

ring

wig

crib

pan

This fish still needs a rhyming picture! On a separate piece of paper, draw something that will rhyme with it. Write the word, too.

Ahoy, mate! It's time to check the map. Look at all these islands! Help us write their names. **Say the picture name of each island. Finish its name by using one of these word families:**

-en   -oin   -ell   -uck

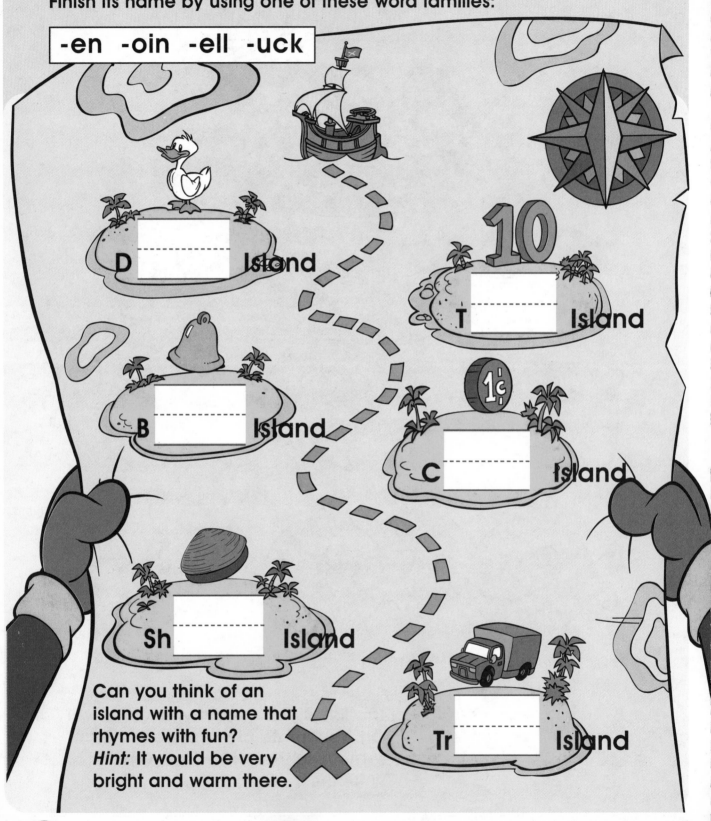

D _____ Island

T _____ Island

B _____ Island

C _____ Island

Sh _____ Island

Tr _____ Island

Can you think of an island with a name that rhymes with fun?
Hint: It would be very bright and warm there.

A ship is a great place to play hide-and-seek. There are big barrels to hide behind. Help me find Floyd. **Look at the pictures on the barrels. Now write in the letters of the word family that makes the sound at the end of each word.**

-ed -in -ap -op -ip -ub -at -ock

Great job! Put your coin sticker on your money sack and jump ahead.

Rhymes and Phonograms 71

Frankie's Facts

Adding a vowel often makes a **long vowel phonogram**. B<u>a</u>t is a **short vowel phonogram**. B<u>oat</u> is a **long vowel phonogram**. A long vowel says its name. You can hear "o" in boat.

Diving dolphins will lead us to Toy Island! **Say the name of the picture on each dolphin. Then fill in the blank with the long a or long o phonogram that finishes the word.**

-ain	-ane	-ate
-oat	-one	-ope

tr _____

b _____

r _____

pl _____

g _____

g _____

Toy Island at last! Time to drop the anchors. **Write the picture names with the long e or long i phonograms under the correct anchor.**

-ean	-ite
-eep	-ice
-eese	-ride
-eal	-ike

long e

_____

s _ _ _ _ _ _ _ _ _ _ _

b _ _ _ _ _ _ _ _ _ _ _

ch _ _ _ _ _ _ _ _ _ _ _

sh _ _ _ _ _ _ _ _ _ _ _

long i

_____

b _ _ _ _ _ _ _ _ _ _ _

b _ _ _ _ _ _ _ _ _ _ _

k _ _ _ _ _ _ _ _ _ _ _

m _ _ _ _ _ _ _ _ _ _ _

Smooth sailing! Put your coin sticker on your money sack and jump ahead!

Let's go ashore! Hop to the first big rock. **Draw a line to the words with the same phonogram. Then hop to the next big rock and do the same thing. Keep going until you reach shore!**

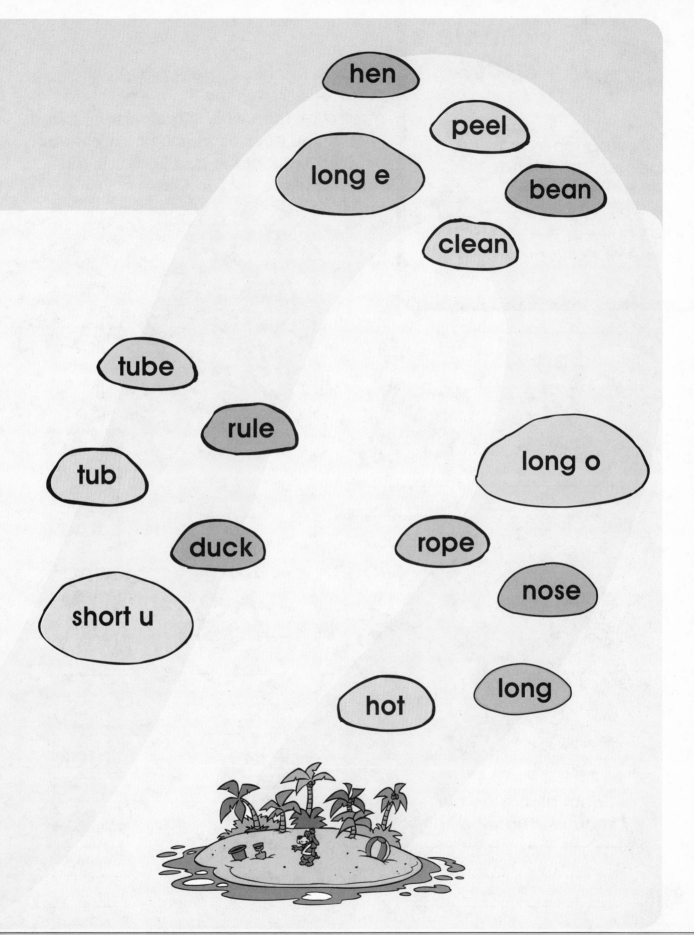

hen

peel

long e

bean

clean

tube

rule

tub

long o

duck

rope

nose

short u

hot

long

Great! Place your dolphin sticker on your Certificate of Completion and jump ahead.

Review 75

Frankie's Facts

Two consonants can work together. They **blend** their sounds. Say this word: s-n-ake. Did you hear the blend of **s** and **n**?

Toy Island has a great playground! While we play, say the name of each picture. **Then write the blends or sounds that you hear at the beginning of each word. Look at the tree leaves if you need clues.**

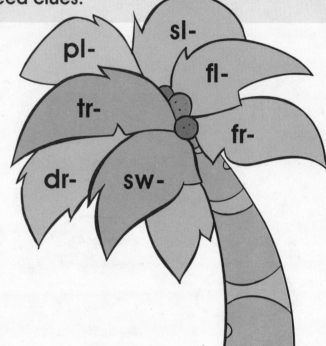

pl-
sl-
fl-
tr-
fr-
dr-
sw-

frog

f r

train

_____

plane

_____

drum

_____

swing

_____

What blends do our names start with?

_____

_____

slide

_____

truck

_____

If you're looking for a toy shop, Toy Island is the place. **Circle the toys that begin with blends. Then underline the letters that make each blend. Write them on the lines.**

train   crab   skate   ball

tiger   pig   sled

plane   seal

Terrific!! Put your coin sticker on your money sack and jump ahead to the next level.

Look at all the balls we found. Floyd wants to shoot some hoops. **See if you can name the two letters that make up the blend in each picture name. Write that blend on the line.**

| st- | sk- | sn- | sl- | sw- |

Find a picture name to which you can add the letter t at the end and get a new word that means begin. Circle it.

The Toy Island Gift shop has lots of jars! Say the picture names of the objects in the jars. Then write the blends you hear at the beginning of each one on the line. Each one is an r-blend.

cr-   gr-   dr-   fr-   tr-

_____ apes

_____ um

_____ ee

_____ own

_____ og

_____ ain

We found a shop that sells flags. We only want to buy the ones that have an "l" sound in the beginning blend. Will you help us? **Circle the pictures with names that start with l-blends.**

Draw your own flag on another piece of paper. Put a picture on it of something that starts with an l-blend.

Yikes! We're stuck in a troop of toy soldiers. Help them back to their guardhouses. **Look at the picture on each of their hats. If the picture name begins with an s-blend, draw a line from the soldier to the s-blend house. Do the same for the r-blend and the l-blend picture names.**

l- blends

s- blends

r- blends

Good for you! Put your coin sticker on your money sack and jump ahead to the next page.

Blends 81

Frankie's Facts

You might also hear a **blend** at the end of a word. Say this word: st-a-mp. Listen to the **mp** blend at the end of the word.

Can you help us win a bowling prize? **Say the picture name on each bowling pin and listen for the sounds at the end. Match each picture name with the correct ball and write the ending blend on the line.**

che _____

a _____

la _____

te _____

ne _____

si _____

(mp) (nt) (st) (st) (nk) (mp)

You won the prize. You are a cha _____ !
(Finish the word with a blend.)

Dog-gone! Here are some piggy banks for saving money. **Put the coins in the banks and see what new words you can make with all the letters you have.**

-am	-mp	-nk
-lt	-sk	-rk

be

belt

bu

cl

pa

ma

ba

You did it! Put your coin sticker on your money sack and jump ahead.

Blends (83)

The Toy Island race cars sure look fast!
Can you get them to the finish line?
**Use the blends on each car to finish the
picture names along the track.
Start your engines!**

START

dr br nt sl

sl nt nd rk br

te _____

_____ eep

_____ ide

_____ oom

ha _____

_____ agon

_____ ush

pai _____

ba _____

fo _____

You were right on track! Place your bracelet sticker on your Certificate of Completion and jump ahead!

Review 85

Frankie's Facts

Sometimes two consonants together stand for one sound. The **s** and the **h** at the end of the word **fish** make one sound. So do the **t** and the **h** at the beginning of **thin**. **Sh** and **th** are **digraphs**.

We've reached Teddy Bear Town. These bears need some color on their shirts. **Say the name of the picture on each shirt. If you hear the beginning sound "sh," color the shirt blue. If you hear the sound "th," color the shirt red.**

Splish! Splash! Everybody jump in! Floyd and I want to share our water toys. **Draw a line from me to the toys that begin with the "ch" sound, like chin. Draw a line from Floyd to the toys that begin with the "wh" sound, like wheel.**

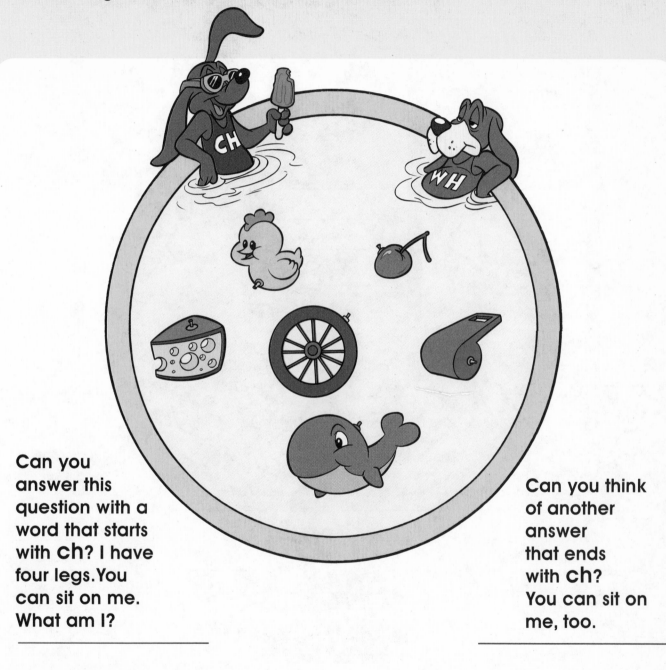

Can you answer this question with a word that starts with ch? I have four legs. You can sit on me. What am I?

_____

Can you think of another answer that ends with ch? You can sit on me, too.

_____

Great job! Put your coin sticker on your money sack and jump ahead to the next level.

Let's take a spin on this Toy Island carousel. First say each picture name out loud. **What two letters make the sound you hear at the beginning? Write those letters on the line.**

I want to ride on a seahorse whose picture name starts with the same sound as **she**. How many choices do I have?

Floyd wants to ride on a seahorse whose picture name starts with the same sound as **chin**. How many choices does he have?

 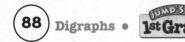

This wall could use some color. Help us paint a picture.
Use a blue crayon to color in all the spaces with words that begin with wh. Who do you see?

How many words begin with the sound of "ch"? _____

How about "sh"? _____

Frankie's Facts

Remember, a **digraph** is two consonants that, when used together, make a new sound, like **sh**ip.

How do we get back to the ship? We need to follow only the paths with blends and digraphs. **Help us find our way by drawing lines that show the four different paths we can take.**

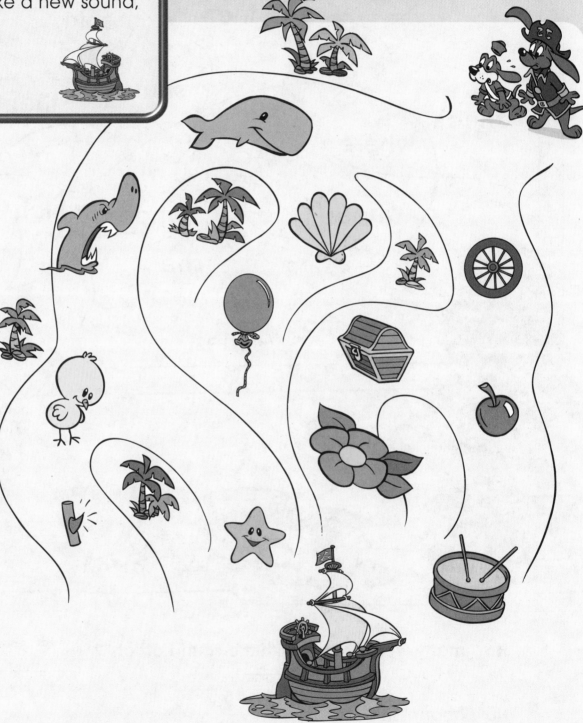

We made it to the shore! Look at all these pails and shovels. Let's take them with us. **Draw a line from each pail to the shovel that completes the picture name. Write the letters on the line.**

umb

ch

est

th

ess

istle

wh

ick

ell

sh

Circle the picture word that might be full of treasures.

Hurray! You did it! Put your coin sticker on your money sack and jump ahead to the next level.

Digraphs **91**

Frankie's Facts

Digraphs can also come at the end of words, like bu**sh**.

Wow! This chest is full of surprises. Find the things that end in digraphs. Say each picture name out loud. Then circle the ones that end in the sounds of "ch," "sh," or "th."

What ends in the sound of "ch," has sand, and is near the sea?

_____

_____

_____

Floyd wants to build sand castles before we ship out.
Help him by using the digraphs in the sand bricks to finish the words.
Some have more than one answer.

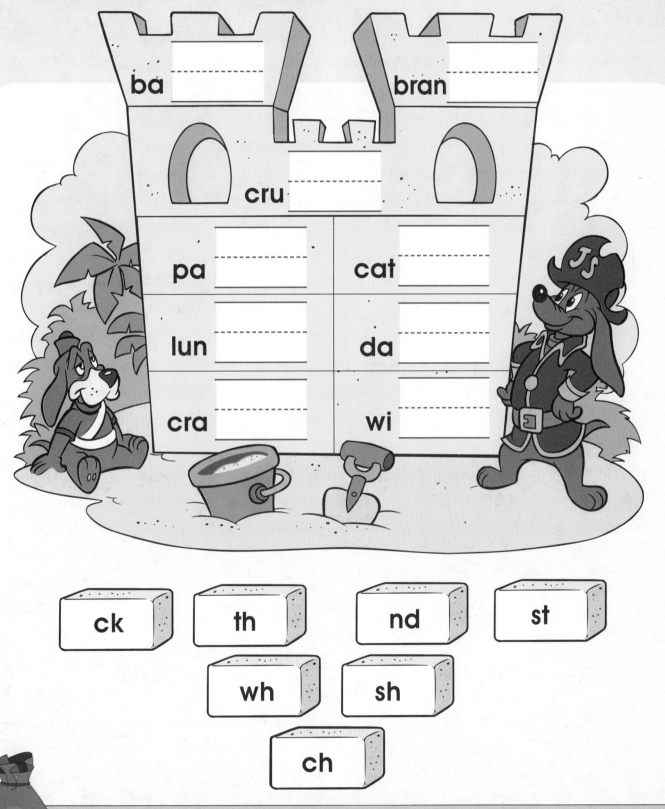

ba _____

bran _____

cru _____

pa _____

cat _____

lun _____

da _____

cra _____

wi _____

ck

th

nd

st

wh

sh

ch

Lift the anchors! We're headed for home. **Sail from island to island by making words with the letters on each island. Write these new words on the lines. Keep going until we reach home!**

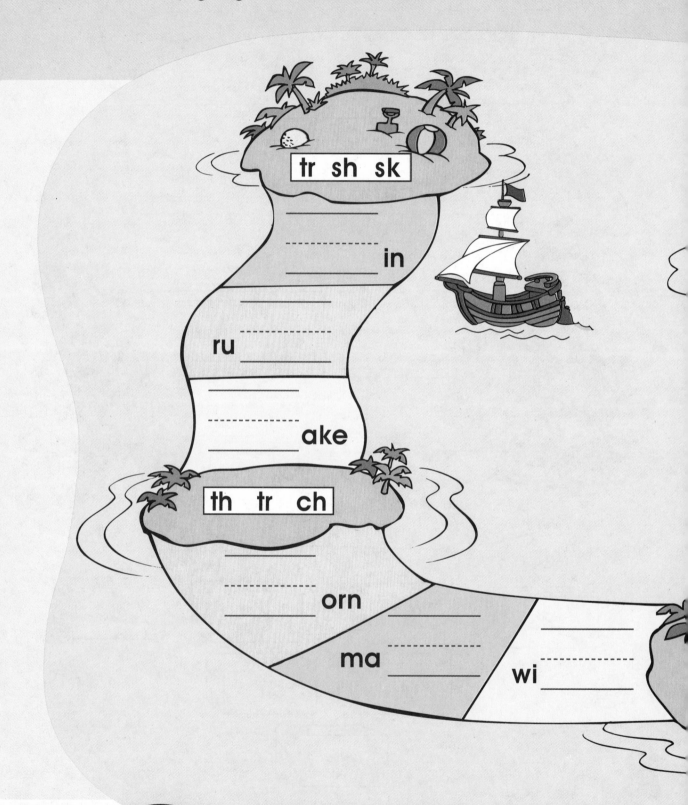

tr sh sk

_____

_____ in

_____

ru _____

_____

_____ ake

th tr ch

_____

_____ orn

_____

ma _____

wi _____

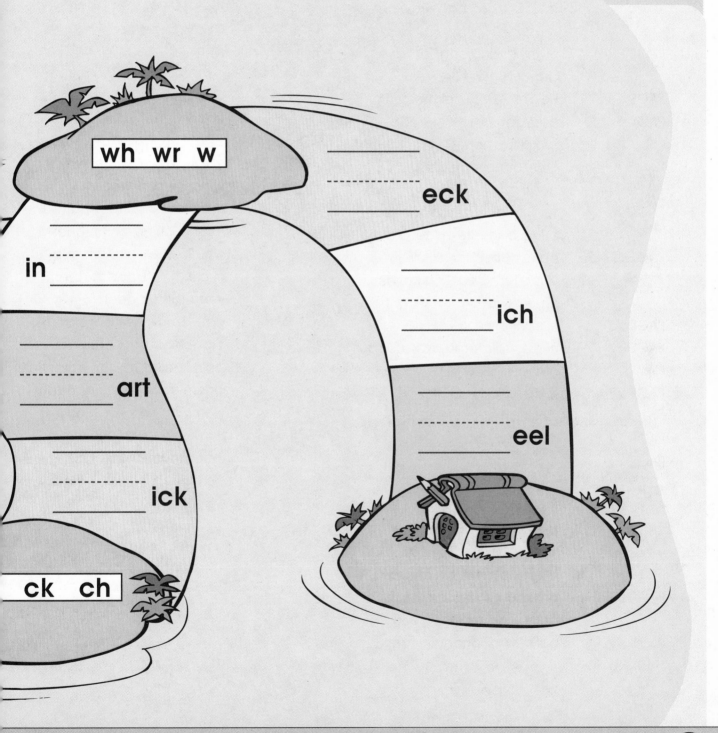

wh wr w

eck

in

ich

art

eel

ick

ck ch

You are the best! You get a jeweled octopus sticker to put on your Certificate of Completion.

Review 95

Answer Key

PAGE 66   cat/rat, hen/pen, fox/box, bug/rug; drawings will vary

PAGE 67   s, h, f, w, m

PAGE 68   man/can, lock/sock, hog/log, cat/bat; drawings will vary

PAGE 69   pig/wig, king/ring, bib/crib; drawings will vary

PAGE 70   uck, en, ell, oin, ell, uck; sun

PAGE 71   bed, cat, pin, block, map, tub, ship, mop

PAGE 72   train, bone, rope, plane, goat, gate

PAGE 73   seal, bean, cheese, sheep; bride, bike, kite, mice

PAGES 74–75   cap, map, pan; six, pin; duck, tub; bean, clean, peel; rope, nose

PAGE 76   tr, pl, dr, sw, sl, tr, Fr, Fl

PAGE 77   circle: train, crab, skate, sled, plane; tr, cr, sk, sl, pl

PAGE 78   sl, st, sn, sk, sw; circle: star/start

PAGE 79   gr, dr, tr, cr, fr, tr

PAGE 80   clam, slipper, globe, glasses, flower; drawings will vary

PAGE 81   [l-blend] clock, glove; [s-blend] spoon, skunk; [r-blend] brush, trumpet

PAGE 82   st, nt, mp, nt, st, nk; champ

PAGE 83   belt; bump or bunk; clam; park; malt, mask, or mark; bank, bark, or bask

PAGES 84–85   sleep, broom, hand, fork, band, paint; tent, slide, brush, dragon

PAGE 86   [color red] thirteen, thumb; [color blue] shoe, shark, shell, shovel

PAGE 87   [lines from Frankie] chicken, cheese, cherry; [lines from Floyd] wheel, whale, whistle; chair; bench or couch

PAGE 88   sh, ch, ch, wh, wh, th, sh; 2, 2

PAGE 89   color: where, white, why, which, when, wheel; 3, 5

PAGE 90   there are 4 correct paths

PAGE 91   thumb, chess, chick, chest, whistle, shell; circle: chest

PAGE 92   circle: brush, peach, teeth, watch, fish; beach

PAGE 93   bath, back, bash, or band; branch; crust or crush; pack, past, or path; catch; lunch; dash; crack or crash; wish, with, wick, or wind

PAGES 94–95   shin or skin, rush, shake; thorn, math, with; chick, chart, inch; wreck, which, wheel

Hi, everyone! It's me, Frankie! I'm always on the lookout for treasure, whether I'm at sea or in town! Let's take a ride through town and find some words to spell.

See these coins? Every time you learn something new, you get one of these stickers to put in your money sack. When you finish each section, you'll get a big treasure sticker to put on your Certificate of Completion at the end of the book.

See this picture of me? When you see it, read what I have to say. It will help you do the work on each page. Just look for **Frankie's Facts**.

Are you ready? Hop aboard!

Frankie's Facts

Many three-letter words are spelled with this pattern:

consonant-vowel-consonant

dog

Let's go! Help me follow the road to the park.

Spell each three-letter word you see and write them on the lines below.

Can you spell the word for what I am riding in?

We'd better get some gas for the bus before we go on.
Look at the pictures on the gas pumps.
Can you spell each three-letter word?
Write the word on the lines.

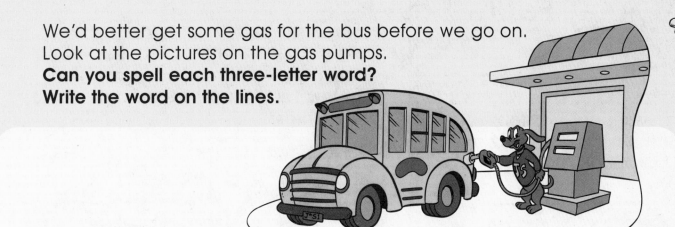

_____
- - - - - - - - - - - - -
_____

_____
- - - - - - - - - - - - -
_____

_____
- - - - - - - - - - - - -
_____

_____
- - - - - - - - - - - - -
_____

_____
- - - - - - - - - - - - -
_____

_____
- - - - - - - - - - - - -
_____

**You did it! Put your coin sticker in
your money sack and jump ahead.**

Frankie's Facts

Some words start with two consonants, like **st**op.
Some words end in two consonants, like sa**ck**.

You have to pay attention to the signs when you ride through town! **Say the picture name on each sign below. Fill in the letters to finish the words.**

__ __ ed   __ __ og   __ __ ib   __ __ ip

du__ __   lo__ __   di__ __

We made it to town! Help me put the names on the street signs.
Say the picture name of each street. Finish its name by writing the missing letters.

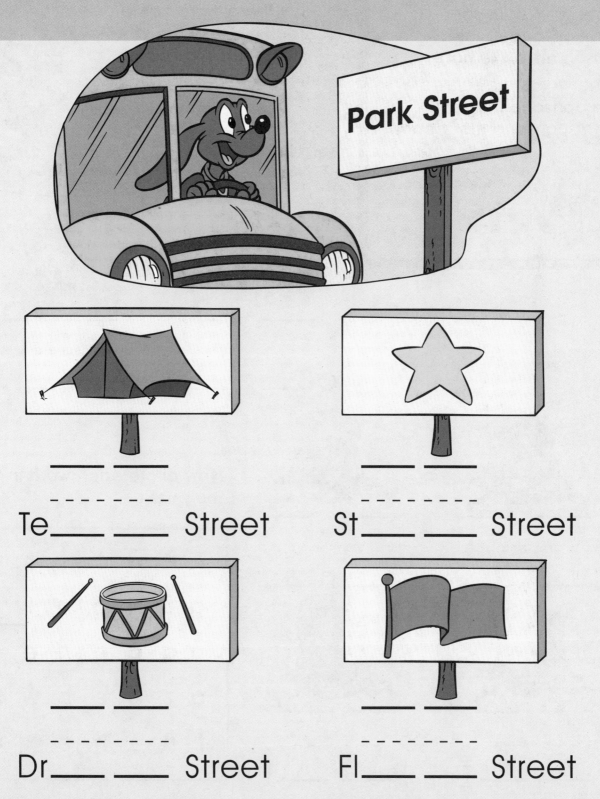

Te_____ Street

St_____ Street

Dr_____ Street

Fl_____ Street

Frankie's Facts

Some words are spelled with **consonant-vowel-consonant-e**, like **hose**.

Some words are spelled with **consonant-vowel-vowel-consonant**, like **coat**.

The town firehouse is a fun place to visit! Do you like my coat and hat?

Say the picture name on each hat. Use the vowels on the hose to finish each word.

i-e   a-e   o-e   ee   oa   ai

c _ n _   p _ _ l

l _ k _   n _ n _

Now circle each word in the puzzle.

g _ _ t   f _ _ t

f	e	e	t	s	r	u
g	r	n	p	a	i	l
o	q	c	o	n	e	a
a	z	c	e	b	w	k
t	n	i	n	e	x	e

It's time to go to the supermarket in town! Floyd gave me a list of things to buy, but the letters are mixed up.
Help me unscramble the words so I can go shopping!

SUPERMA

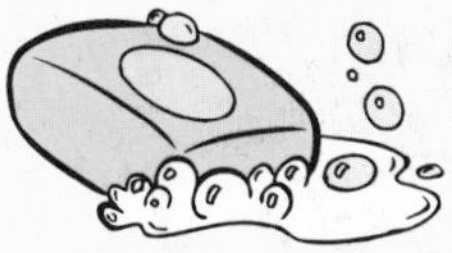

o n r c _____

p a s o _____

k a c e _____

l k m i _____

c i e r _____

Great job! Put your coin sticker in the money sack and jump ahead!

I'm looking for a dog, a bear, a fox, a pig, and an ant.
Can you help me?
**Find and circle them in the picture. Then read
each sentence below. Unscramble the words
to complete each sentence.**

That dog likes to smile. That dog is very _____.
(a p p y h)

The bear is very big. The bear is _____.
(a r l e g)

That pig can _____ a car.
(v i d r e)

That fox can _____ from a cup.
(d n k r i)

That ant is tiny. It is a very _____ ant.
(l l a m s)

Let's spell some more words together!

Color the picture. Then read each sentence and write the missing word on the line. Look in the picture for clues.

A _____ tells you what time it is.

A _____ has four wheels.

A _____ moves along a track.

A _____ flies in the sky.

A _____ has a bad smell.

The number _____ comes before the number four.

That's great! Put your coin sticker in your money sack and jump ahead!

There are so many great stores in town! Help me visit each one.

R_____ Store

Dr_____s Shop

P_____nt Store

_____ate Shop

_____i___e Shop

Fill in the missing letters on each store sign.

K___t___ Shop

_____ant Store

Fi_____ Shop

_____g Shop

_____irt Shop

_____amp Shop

You win! Place your big bottle sticker on your Certificate of Completion. Then jump ahead!

Review (107)

Frankie's Facts

Sight words are words that we see a lot. You can recognize them quickly, so you don't have to sound them out.

Here we are at the zoo! Help me find some sight words.
When you see one of these words in the story below, draw a circle around it.

the	is	a	I	you	we	and

This is the Zippy Zoo.

The Zippy Zoo is a clean and nice zoo.

We want you to talk to the birds and the fish.

This is what we want you to say:

"Hello, I am happy that we are at the

Zippy Zoo."

Wow! Five monkeys are hiding here.
Write one of the words from the box on each line to complete the sentences. Some sentences have more than one answer.

the
is
a
I
we

_____

The - - - - - - - - - -
_____ in a bush.

_____

The is behind - - - - - - - - - -
_____ rock.

_____

- - - - - - - - - -

_____ are side by side.

_____

- - - - - - - - - -

_____ see a with a flower.

_____

- - - - - - - - - -

I wish Floyd were here. Then _____ could play.

Good work! Put your coin sticker in your money sack and jump ahead.

Sight Words 109

Look at all the seals!

Read the signs and circle the words from the box. Then draw a line from the sign to the matching seal.

are   on   not   has   do   to   a

Do not sit on
the rock with
this seal.

This seal
likes
to dive.

This seal
has
a ball.

This seal
has
a fish.

These two
seals are
brothers.

Let's get back on the bus and go to the library! The red line on my map shows the road we will follow.
Follow the path, starting at the word "zoo." When you come to a word, write it on the line in the sentences below. The word order on the map matches the word order in the sentences.

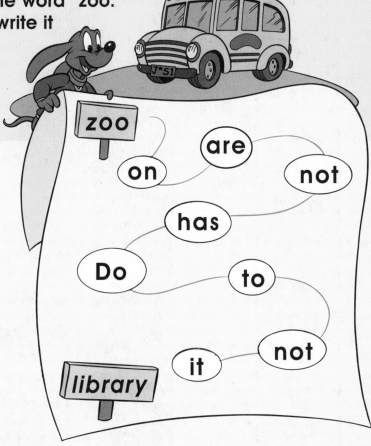

Go! The ducks are _____ **on** _____ the lake now.

Stop! There _____ two little ducks in the road.

Do _____ stop here.

The monkey _____ gone away.

_____ not feed an apple _____ the snake.

The snake will _____ like _____!

Wow! I can't wait to read these books! They're full of sight words. **Look on the book covers for the words in the box. Draw a circle around each one that you find.**

the
is
a
I
and
are
on
not
do
to
no
it

The Cats and Dogs Are on the Moon

A Worm Is Not a Lion

How to Do a Fast Dance

A Funny Pig

No, I Will Not Be It This Time!

A Toad Is Bumpy

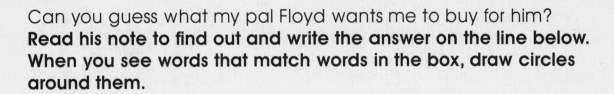

Can you guess what my pal Floyd wants me to buy for him?
Read his note to find out and write the answer on the line below.
When you see words that match words in the box, draw circles around them.

Please go to the toy store. No, I do not want a game, and I do not want a toy car. I want something to play with. It is round. We like to bounce it and throw it. The store on King Street has it.

It is a _____!

the	not
is	has
a	do
I	to
we	no
and	it

Terrific job! Put your coin sticker in your money sack and jump ahead.

Sight Words (113)

Can you help me read these signs?
Read each sentence below. Write each word from the box on the correct sign.

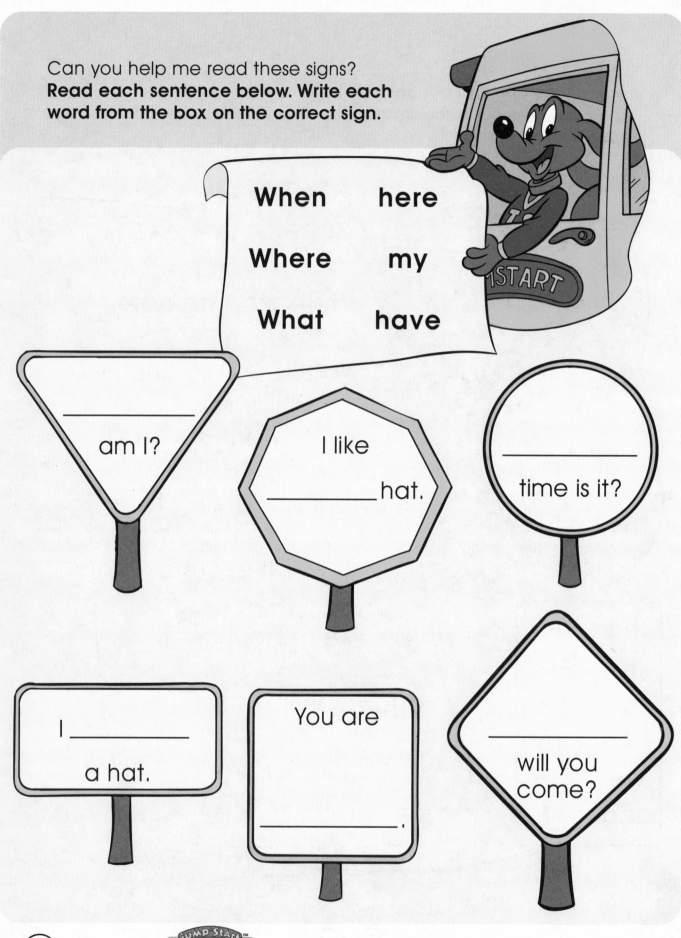

When   here

Where   my

What   have

_____
am I?

I like
_____ hat.

_____
time is it?

I _____
a hat.

You are

_____.

_____
will you come?

Here we are in the toy store!
**Read each sentence and look for the missing word on the balls.
Then write the words that complete each sentence on the
lines below.**

This   too   play

go   see

I like to
_____
_____
ball.

_____
- - - - - - -
Let's_____
to the park.

_____
- - - - - - - -
_____
is my friend.

My
friend likes
to play ball,
_____
- - - - - - -
_____ .

I will
_____
- - - - - - -
_____
you there!

**Excellent! Put your coin sticker in
your money sack and jump ahead!**

Sight Words (115)

I want to play on the slide in the park. Will you come, too?
Help me find the right road.

This
is
where
go
we
no   not   do
on
this
road.
Where   are   we?

Read the word on each stone.
Follow the path that makes four
complete sentences and color it in!

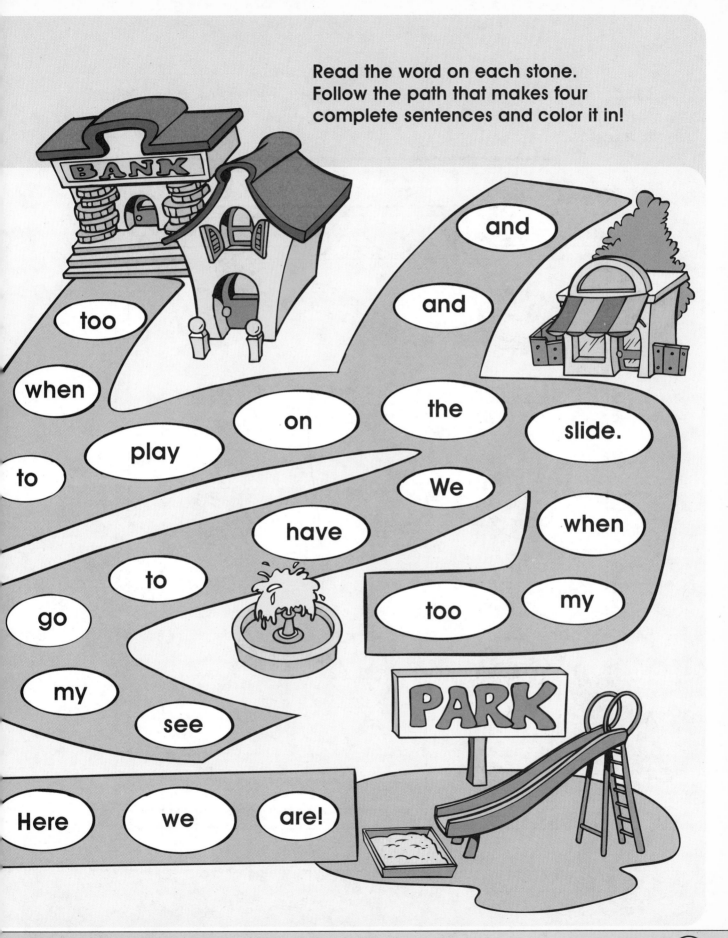

too

when

play

on

the

and

and

slide.

We

when

to

have

go

to

too

my

my

see

Here   we   are!

PARK

BANK

Good for you! Place your royal robe sticker on your
Certificate of Completion and jump ahead.

Review 117

Everything in this store needs a beginning letter!
Read the word ending under each picture. Then pick a first letter from the box to complete the word. Some letters are used more than once.

h   f   b   p   j   c

___at   ___at   ___in

___it   ___an   ___an

___am   ___an   ___in

Can you help me untangle these balloons?
Read the word at the bottom of each string. Then follow the string with your finger and write the missing letters to finish the matching word. Color the balloons.

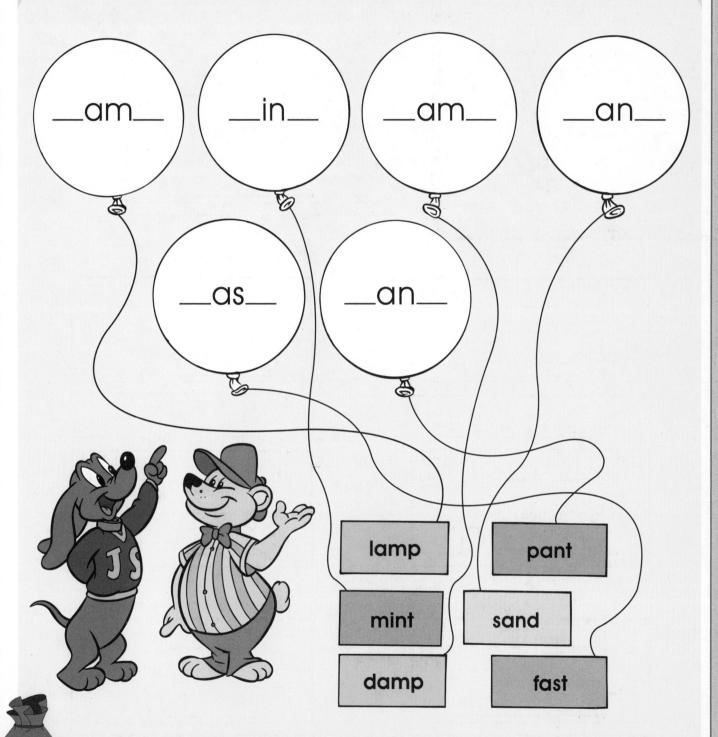

__am__   __in__   __am__   __an__

__as__   __an__

lamp   pant

mint   sand

damp   fast

**You did it! Put your coin sticker in
your money sack and jump ahead.**

Frankie's Facts

Add letters to the beginning or end of a word and make a new word! Did you know that adding an **e** to the end of a word makes the whole word sound different?

cap

cape

Here we are in the post office! What words belong on the envelopes? **Read the clues and do the word math. Write the word on each envelope.**

tap + e =

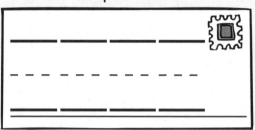

wish – wi =

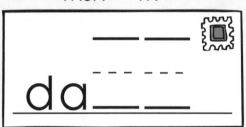
da _ _ _ _

slide - e =

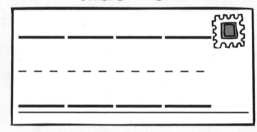

seal – al =

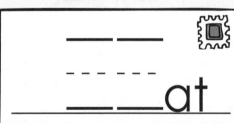
_ _ _ at

trip – tr =

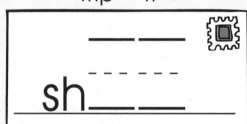
sh _ _ _ _

sink – s =

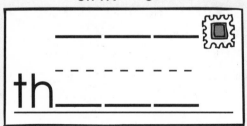
th _ _ _ _ _

wish – sh =

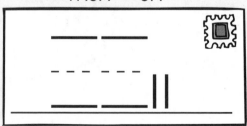
_ _ _ ll

Let's climb up this building! The words all change a little as you climb. **Color in each word path from the brick at the bottom to the brick at the top. Use a different color for all five paths. One vowel in each path will not change.**

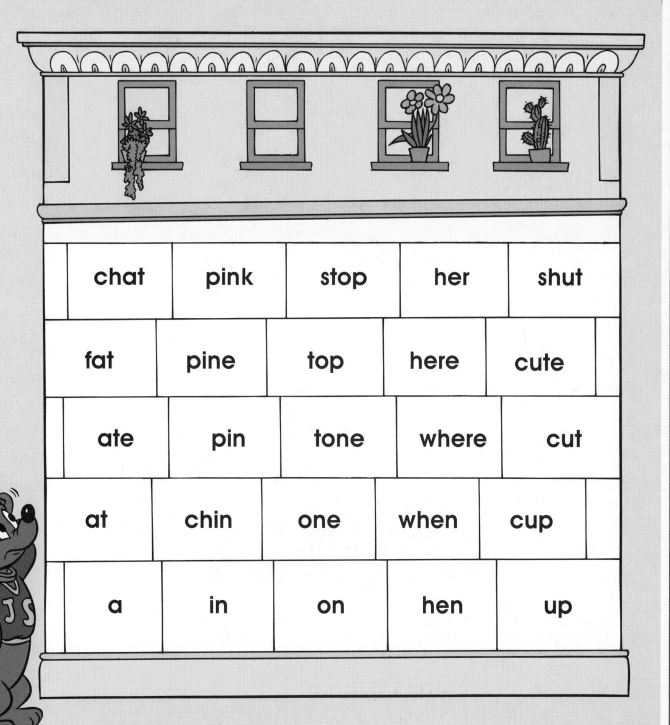

chat	pink	stop	her	shut
fat	pine	top	here	cute
ate	pin	tone	where	cut
at	chin	one	when	cup
a	in	on	hen	up

Look at what's growing in this garden! Let's grow some words!
Make words on each petal using the blends in the center of each flower. Write the letters on the lines to make each new word.

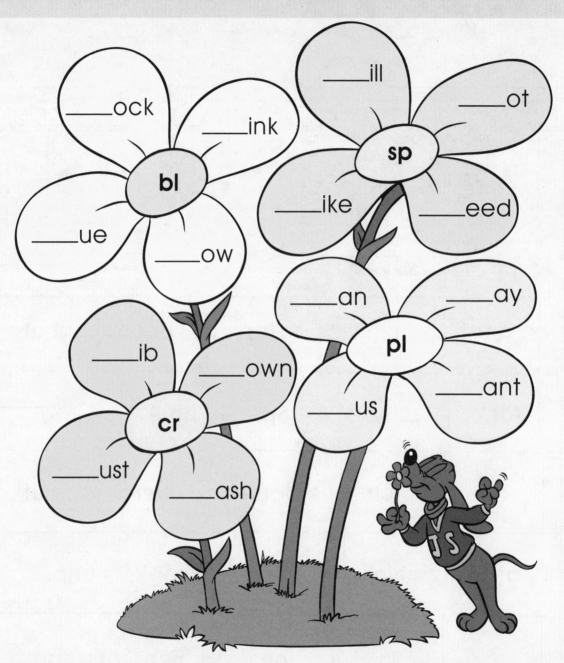

Can you make up some words on your own using these blends?

bl_____   sp_____

cr_____   pl_____

I wonder what movie is coming to the theater!

Look at the letters at the top of each column. Write them at the beginning or end of each word underneath.

sh	**ch**	**th**	**wh**
___ake	wat___	___ink	___ale
wa___	ri___	ba___	___at
___op	___ip	___ick	___ich

Make up a funny name for the movie!
Use some of the words you wrote.
Write the name of the movie on the line at the top of the page.

Good for you! Put your coin sticker in your money sack and jump ahead.

There's something funny about the trees in town. I think they're growing words!

Use the letters in the box to make words with the word endings on each tree. You can use more than one letter from the box in a single word. Write the words on the lines.

l m r b c h f s w

___ink

___ake

___ang

rink

blink

Let's build words!

Draw lines between the matching endings. Then write a letter on each line to make a new word.

___eat   ___rip

___and   ___ate

___rip   ___eat

___ate   ___and

Excellent! Put your coin sticker in your money sack and jump ahead.

Word Building **125**

It's been lots of fun visiting town. Before we go home, do you want to play a game with me?

___at   ___a   ___an

___nk   ___ink   ___ay

___ock   ___ock   ___old

___ank   ___ank   ___ame

Write a letter on each line to make a new word. You'll have a whole book full when you're finished!

____an   ____ip   ____ip

____ay   ____ash   ____ash

____old   ____ing   ____ing

____ame   ____ame   ____op

Hooray! You did it! Place your big necklace sticker on your Certificate of Completion!

Review (127)

Answer Key

PAGE 98   write cat, dog, sun, mop, cup, pig; write bus

PAGE 99   write map, fan, rug, fox, can, log

PAGE 100   write sl, fr, cr, sh, ck, ck, sh

PAGE 101   write nt, ar, um, ag

PAGE 102   write o e, ai, a e, i e, oa, ee; circle feet, pail, cone, nine, goat, lake

PAGE 103   write corn, soap, cake, milk, rice

PAGE 104   circle (in picture) dog, bear, fox, pig, ant; write happy, large, drive, drink, small

PAGE 105   write clock, truck, train, plane, skunk, three

PAGES 106–107   write ug, es, ai, i e, Pl, sh, Sk, B k, Wi, Sh, St

PAGE 108   circle (first line) is, the, (second line) The, is, a, and, (third line) We, you, the, and, the, (fourth line) is, we, you, (fifth line) I, we, the

PAGE 109   write (first line) is, (second line) a or the, (third line) The or We, (fourth line) I or We, (fifth line) I or we

PAGE 110   circle (clockwise from top) sign 1/do, not, on; sign 2/has, a; sign 3/are; sign 4/has, a; sign 5/to; connect sign 1/seal sitting on rock, sign 2/seal balancing ball on nose, sign 3/pair of seals in center of pool, sign 4/seal with fish in mouth, sign 5/seal diving

PAGE 111   write are, not, has, Do, to, not, it

PAGE 112   (from left to right) circle Book 1/The, and, are, on, the; Book 2/A, is, Not, a; Book 3/to, Do, a; Book 4/a; Book 5/No, I, Not, It; Book 6/A, Is

PAGE 113   circle to, the, No, I, do, not, a, and, I, do, not, a, I, to, It, is, We, to, it, and, it, The, on, has, it, It, is, a; ball

PAGE 114   write Where, my, What, have, here, When

PAGE 115   write play, go, This, too, see

PAGES 116–117   color the path that reads This is where we go to play on the slide. We have to go on this road. Where are we? Here we are!

PAGE 118   write h, b, f, p, p, c, j, f, p

PAGE 119   write l p, m t, d p, s d, f t, p t

PAGE 120   write (top) tape, (left column) dash, seat, think, (right column) slid, ship, will

PAGE 121   color a, at, ate, fat, chat; in, chin, pin, pine, pink; on, one, tone, top, stop; hen, when, where, here, her; up, cup, cut, cute, shut

PAGE 122   write four times each bl, sp, cr, pl; answers will vary

PAGE 123   write three times each sh, ch, th, wh; answers will vary

PAGE 124   write blink, brink, chink, clink, fink, link, mink, rink, slink, sink, or wink; write bake, brake, cake, fake, flake, lake, make, rake, sake, shake, slake, or wake; write bang, clang hang, fang, rang, sang, or slang

PAGE 125   connect eat/eat, and/and, rip/rip, ate/ate; answers will vary

PAGES 126–127   answers will vary

Hi! It's Frankie here! My pal Floyd and I are on our way to the beach. Why don't you come along? We'll have lots of fun in the sun!

See these coin stickers? Every time you learn something new, you get a sticker for your money sack. When you finish each section, you get a great big sticker for your Certificate of Completion at the end of the book.

One more thing! When you see this picture of me, it means that I'm there to help you. Just look for **Frankie's Facts**.

We're off to the beach! I wonder what we'll find there!

WELCOME

Frankie's Facts

Nouns are words that name people, places, or things.

Frankie is at the **beach** holding a **shell**.

Hi, there! It's time for a great day at the beach. While we look around, help us sort the nouns. **Circle our names. Underline each noun that names a thing.**

Floyd

ship

hat

pail

Frankie

towel

shell

Skywriting is fun to watch, but these words are all mixed up.
Circle the three nouns in the sky.

FLYING

AIRPLANE

A

THE

BIRD

AN

IS

LITTLE

AND   WEARING

HAT

Now help me make one big sentence using the nouns you circled.

The little _____ is wearing a _____

and flying an _____ .

Great job! Place your coin sticker in
your money sack and jump ahead.

Nouns & Pronouns

131

Let's get our ship so we can go for a sail. **Help us by writing the correct noun in each sentence below. Look at the picture for clues.**

1. A _____ is in the water.

2. An airplane is in the _____.

3. A car is on the _____.

4. A bird is in the _____.

5. Floyd and I want a ride to the ship. Maybe

   the _____ will give us a ride on his back!

It looks like rain. Before we go inside, let's sort the nouns. **Circle my name. Then read and underline the nouns that name people or things.**

house

cloudy

ship

girl   the

baby

are

cup   peach

boy

bag   towel   dish

Frankie

There are three paths in the sand. I wonder which one we should follow. Read the words in each path. **One of these paths has the words you will need to complete each sentence below. Write them on the lines. Then color the path.**

1. It's fun to go to the _____.

2. When you walk, you sink into the _____.

3. If you get hot, you can cool off in the _____.

4. You dry off with a _____.

5. If you get hungry, you can eat _____.

6. If you get sleepy, you can take a _____.

It's a good thing the trail led to Jill's Place. We're hungry!
While Jill fixes our lunch, let's play a game. **Circle all the nouns.**
Then write the correct noun in each sentence below.

1. _____ is working hard.

2. I will have grape _____ to drink.

3. Floyd will drink _____.

4. Jill will put our food on the _____.

5. While we eat, each of us will sit on a _____.

**Mmm! That was good! Place your coin sticker
in your money sack and jump ahead.**

Nouns & Pronouns (135)

Frankie's Facts

When we talk or write about a person, place, or thing, we don't always say its name. We can use a **pronoun** instead. A **pronoun** is a word that can take the place of a noun.

Floyd is my pal.
He is my pal.

It's stopped raining now. Look at those birds holding pronouns! **Draw a line from each noun in the picture to the pronoun that means the same thing. Then color in each bird.**

he   she   it

umbrella

girl

sister

boy

towel

blanket

These pronouns are flying high! **To finish each sentence, find the correct pronoun on a kite. Write it on the line.**

1. A girl is flying a kite. _____ is flying a kite.

2. A boy is flying a kite. _____ is flying a kite.

3. No one is flying the third kite. _____ is flying away.

Brilliant job! Place your coin sticker in your money sack and jump ahead.

We're collecting shells! I want to pick up the shells with nouns, and Floyd wants to pick up the shells with pronouns. **Color all the noun shells red and the pronoun shells blue.**

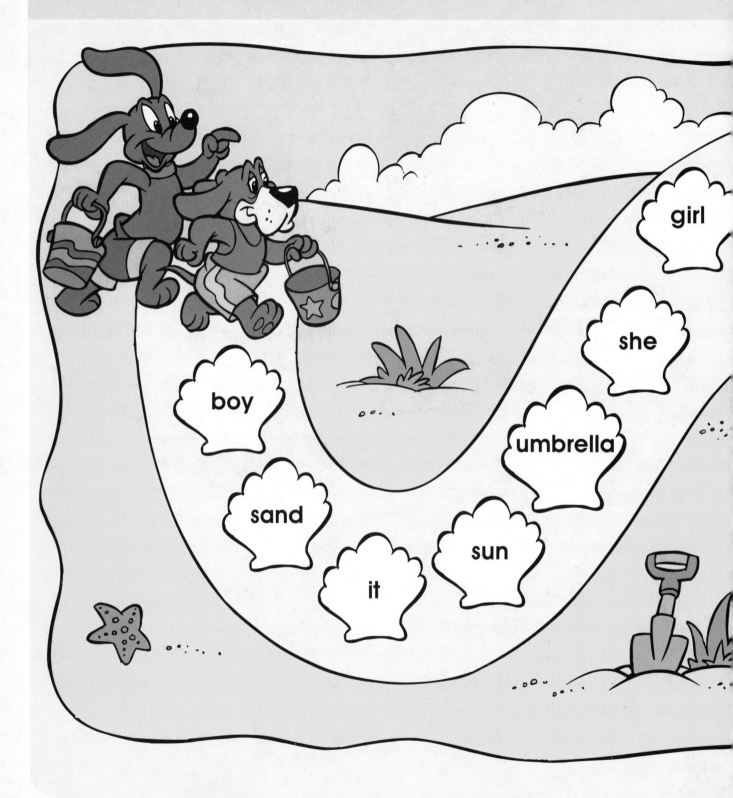

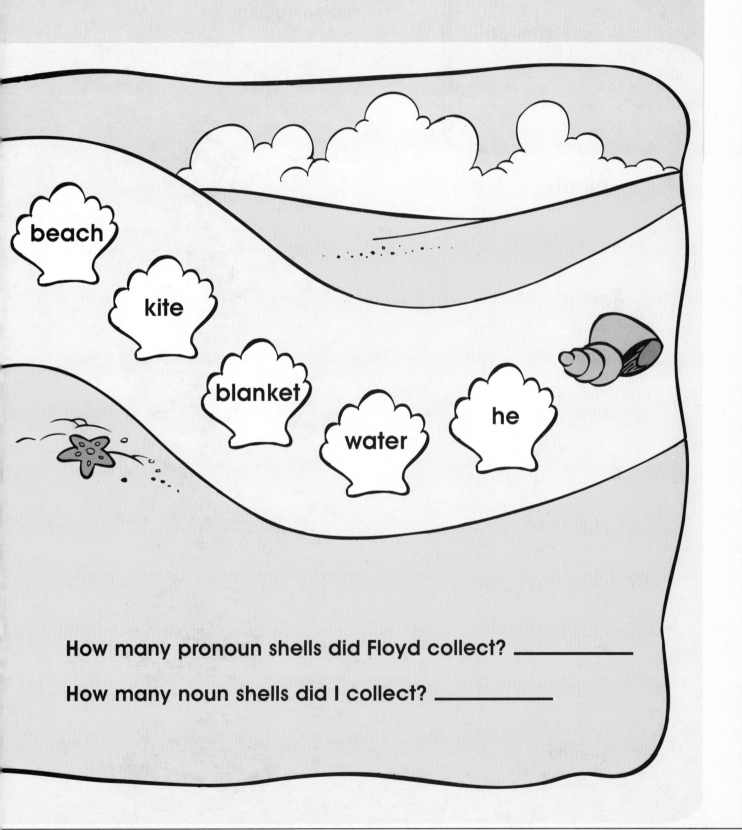

beach

kite

blanket

water

he

How many pronoun shells did Floyd collect? _____

How many noun shells did I collect? _____

Excellent! Place your silverware sticker on your
Certificate of Completion and jump ahead.

Review 139

Frankie's Facts

A **verb** is an **action word**. It tells you what is being done.

Walk, **read**, and **run** are all verbs.

Floyd is having a busy day!
Draw lines between the verbs and the matching pictures.

climb

swim

throw

run

jump

sleep

Let's play ball on the beach! Look at the baseball players and find the verb that describes each one. **Choose from the words in the baseballs and write the correct words on the lines.**

run   catch   jump   hide   hit   slide

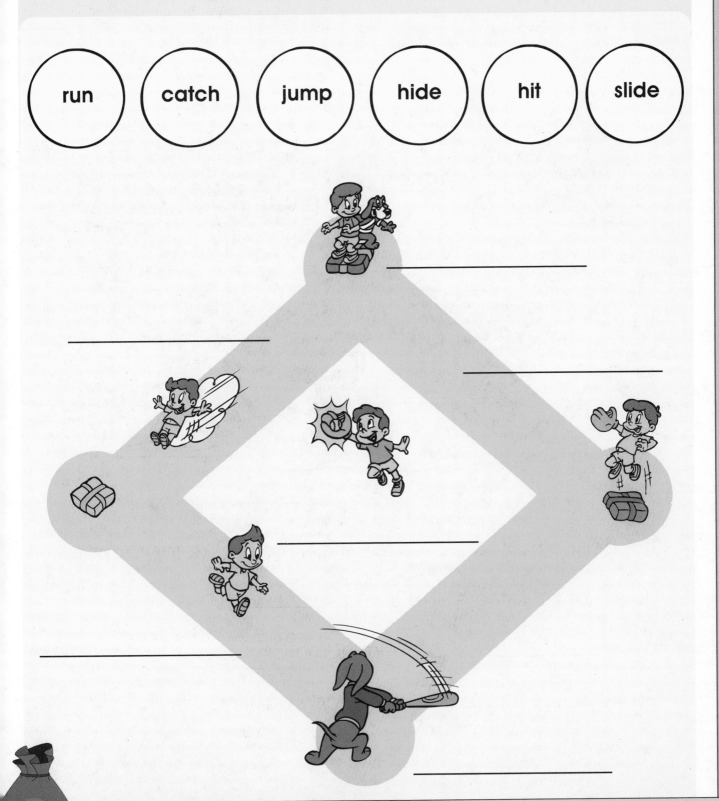

You did it! Place your coin sticker in your money sack and jump ahead.

It's raining verb beach balls! You can help Floyd and me catch them. **Read each sentence. Then fill in the blank with a verb from one of the beach balls.**

fall   take   catch   count

The beach balls _____ from the sky like raindrops.

How many are there? Let's _____.

We can _____ them home!

Help me _____ the beach balls.

Someone wrote a message in the sand. **First, draw circles around the verbs as you read each hint. Then write your answer on the line. Look at the picture for clues!**

I never eat hay.

I never bark.

I never say meow.

I sing and fly most of the time.

Sometimes I write in the sand.

Can you guess who I am?

_____

Frankie's Facts

You can also use **verbs** when you tell somebody to do something.

Stay. Go. Sit. Stand.

Floyd and I are playing follow the leader. Each sentence below is part of the game. Help Floyd follow me. **Circle the verb in each sentence.**

1. Raise your hands.

2. Hop on one foot.

3. Stand still.

4. Close your eyes.

5. Count to ten.

6. Flap your arms like a bird.

7. Jump in the sand.

8. Pretend you are asleep.

Now it's your turn. Try doing each one of these things yourself!

Floyd is busy! Let's help him keep going.
Fill in the blank in each sentence with a verb from the word box.

| Swing | Climb | Jump |
| Balance | Ride | Carry |

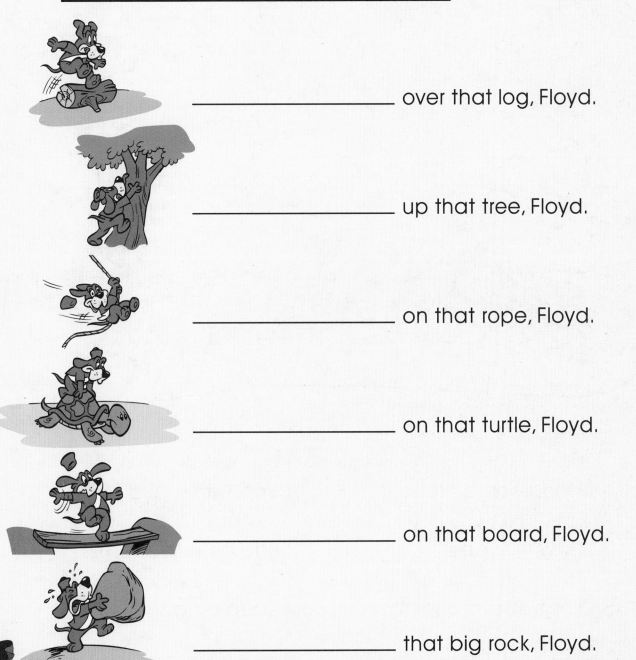

_____ over that log, Floyd.

_____ up that tree, Floyd.

_____ on that rope, Floyd.

_____ on that turtle, Floyd.

_____ on that board, Floyd.

_____ that big rock, Floyd.

Great! Place your coin sticker in your money sack and jump ahead.

Verbs (145)

There are lots of things happening in my dream! **Read the sentences and draw a circle around each verb. Then color in the shapes.**

1. I dance on a cloud.

2. I fly with a bee.

3. I float above a rainbow.

4. I sing with a bird.

5. I ride on a spaceship.

6. I sleep on a star.

Help me surf through all of these words. **Follow the path and decide whether each word is a noun or a verb. Each time you read a verb, write on a line below.**

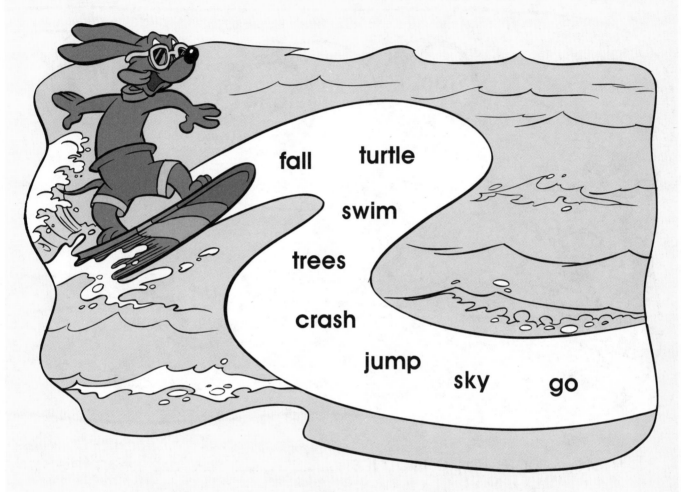

fall   turtle
swim
trees
crash
jump   sky   go

I will not _____ fall _____ into the water.

Maybe I'll _____ with a fish!

I hope I won't _____ into a whale.

How high can I _____?

How far can I _____?

Excellent job! Place your coin sticker in your money sack and jump ahead.

How about a game of ball?

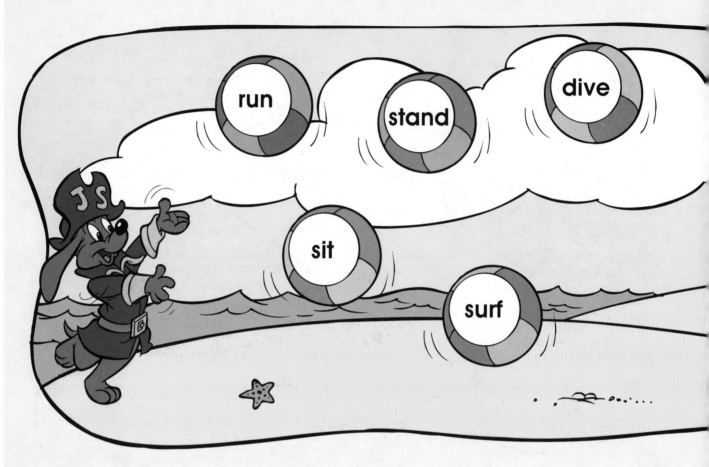

1. There is more to do than just _____ in the sand.

2. Now, _____ up and get moving!

3. You can _____ in the water.

4. If you have a board, you can _____.

5. It's hard to _____, because you sink in the sand.

Read the sentences below. Fill in the blanks with a word from one of the balls. Some sentences have more than one correct answer.

6. You can _____ deeply with a shovel.

7. No matter how high you _____ you can't

reach the sky.

8. _____ that ball to me.

9. Now it's time to _____.

10. If you're tired, you can _____.

You're a winner! Place your statue sticker on your Certificate of Completion and jump ahead.

Review 149

Frankie's Facts

An **adjective** is a word that describes. It can also tell how many or what color.

Here are **three small, purple** shells.

Floyd and I found some seashells. Help us count the shells in each pile. **Draw a line from each pile to the correct box in the middle of the page. Then color the pile the correct color.**

| **one** **black** shell |
| **four** **purple** shells |
| **seven** **pink** shells |
| **two** **blue** shells |
| **nine** **brown** shells |
| **ten** **orange** shells |

This beach needs some more color! Can you help?
Read the sentences below and follow the directions.

Color two shells brown.

Color one shell purple.

Color three shells blue.

Color four shells pink.

Color the last shell any color you like.

**Wonderful! Place your coin sticker in
your money sack and jump ahead.**

Frankie's Facts

An **adjective** can describe how something looks or feels.

Dog-gone! I lost my red hat. Help me follow the trail of hats to find it. **Read each sentence. Put an X on the hat it describes.**

Start at the **tiny** hat.
Now find the **old** hat.
Find the **big** hat.
Go to the **happy** hat.
Climb the tree to get to the **fancy** hat.
Slide down the **long** hat.
What do you see? Circle it.

Floyd wants to tell me about his new friends. Can you help him find the right words to describe them? **Read the adjectives on the kites. Then draw lines from each kite tail to the animal that kite describes.**

happy   sleepy   long   tall   sad

We brought some snacks for a picnic.
Draw lines from each snack to the adjective that describes it.

many

long

huge

purple

frosted

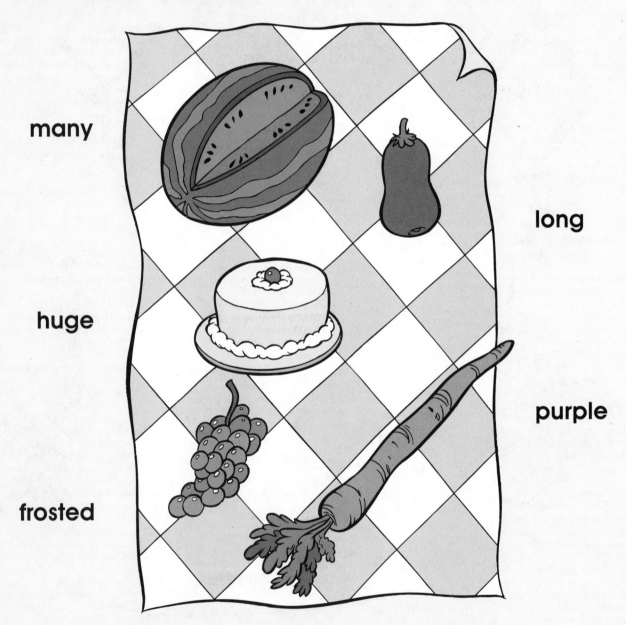

Will you help me get through this maze of towels to my own towel? **Draw a path from towel to towel in this order: striped, old, purple, square, green, small.**

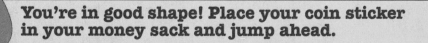

You're in good shape! Place your coin sticker in your money sack and jump ahead.

We need your help to finish our sand castle. **Read the sentences below and underline all the adjectives. Some sentences have more than one adjective. Then follow the directions.**

Draw a large square door on the castle.

Add two little windows above the door.

Draw a short tower on top of the castle.

Draw a narrow bridge leading toward the door.

Let's play one more game! Who will be on my blue team? Who will be on Floyd's red team? **Read the sentences below. Circle all the adjectives. Then color in the rabbits' shirts and flags red or blue.**

The old rabbit is on the blue team.

The sleepy rabbit is on the red team.

The tall gray rabbit is on the red team.

The baby rabbit is on the blue team.

The spotted rabbit is on the blue team.

The noisy rabbit is on the red team.

Excellent! Place your coin sticker in your money sack and jump ahead.

Adjectives (157)

It's time to go home! Our ship is waiting. Let's use adjectives to help us pack up. **Read the list below and help us find our missing things in the picture. Circle them.**

six yellow

two wooden

happy

two round

two pink

purple

striped

Excellent job! Place your rubies sticker on your Certificate of Completion. You did it!

Answer Key

PAGE 130	circle Frankie, Floyd; underlin ship, hat, pail, towel, shell
PAGE 131	circle airplane, bird, hat; write bird, hat, airplane
PAGE 132	1. ship, 2. sky, 3. sand, 4. tree, 5. turtle
PAGE 133	circle Frankie; underline house, ship, girl, baby, peach, cup, dish, bag, towel, boy
PAGE 134	1. beach, 2. sand, 3. water, 4. towel, 5. lunch, 6. nap; color third path
PAGE 135	circle hot dogs, Jill, bananas, wall, chips, cookies, counter, stool, juice, milk; 1. Jill, 2. juice, 3. milk, 4. counter, 5. stool
PAGE 136	connect umbrella/it, girl/she, sister/she, boy/he, blanket/it, towel/it
PAGE 137	1. She, 2. He, 3. It, 4. it
PAGES 138–139	color (red) boy, sand, sun, umbrella, girl, beach, kite, blanket, water; color (blue) it, she, he; 3; 9
PAGE 140	connect verbs/matching pictures
PAGE 141	write (top to bottom) hide, slide, jump, catch, run, hit
PAGE 142	write fall, count, take, catch
PAGE 143	circle eat, bark, say, sing, fly, write; write, a/the bird
PAGE 144	circle Raise, Hop, Stand, Close, Count, Flap, Jump, Pretend
PAGE 145	write Jump, Climb, Swing, Ride, Balance, Carry
PAGE 146	circle dance, fly, float, sing, ride, sleep; color shapes
PAGE 147	write, swim, crash, jump, go
PAGES 148–149	1. run, sit, stand, jump, or dig; 2. sit, stand, or jump; 3. run, sit, stand, surf, dive, or jump; 4. surf; 5. run, stand, or jump; 6. dig; 7. jump, 8. Throw; 9. any of the word choices; 10. sit or sleep
PAGE 150	connect piles to boxes by the correct number; color shells to match
PAGE 151	color two shells brown, one shell purple, three shells blue, four shells pink; color of last shell will vary
PAGE 152	X on all hats except Frankie's; circle Frankie's hidden hat
PAGE 153	connect happy/pig, sleepy/ elephant, long/snake, tall/giraffe, sad/cat
PAGE 154	connect watermelon/huge, eggplant/purple, cake/frosted, grapes/many, carrot/long
PAGE 155	connect towels striped, old, purple, square, green, small to FRANKIE towel
PAGE 156	draw large square door, two small windows above door, short tower on top of castle, bridge over moat
PAGE 157	circle old, blue; sleepy, red; tall, gray, red; baby, blue; spot ted, blue; noisy, red; color (blue) old rabbit, baby rabbit, spotted rabbit; color (red) sleepy rabbit, tall rabbit, rabbit with drum
PAGES 158–159	circle six yellow flowers, two wooden airplanes, one balloon with smiling face and Frankie, two round balls, two pink shells, one purple towel, one striped towel

Ahoy! It's Captain Frankie here. Floyd and I are on the way to Fairy Tale Island to look for treasure. Do you like to read? A book is just like a treasure — full of adventure and fun. Hang on! Here we go!

See these coin stickers? Every time you finish learning something new, you get one of these stickers to put in your money sack. When you finish a whole section, you'll get a big sticker to put in your special treasure chest on the Certificate of Completion at the end of this book.

See this picture of me? When you see it on the page, it means I'm there to give you a little help. Just look for **Frankie's Facts**.

Now, let's not waste another minute. Ahoy, mates!

Frankie's Facts

Some words, such as **little** and **small**, mean the same thing. They are called **synonyms**. Other words, such as **stop** and **go**, mean the opposite. They are called **antonyms**.

Fairy Tale Island at last! I don't see any treasure, but I spot some of the fairy-tale characters. **Look at each pair of characters and read the words under them. If the words are opposites, color the circles red. If they are the same, color the circles blue.**

fast   slow

run   jog

large   small

big   little

girl   boy

happy   glad

Wow! The characters on this island really are right out of fairy tales! How would you describe them? **Under the picture, there are pairs of words missing their first two letters. If you fill them in, you will have words that mean the same. Look in the word box for help.**

happy	thin	skinny	little	big	pretty
large	glad	angry	small	mad	beautiful

__ __ rge	__ __ g
__ __ d	__ __ gry
__ __ inny	__ __ in

__ __ etty	__ __ autiful
__ __ ad	__ __ ppy
__ __ all	__ __ ttle

No treasure here. But Goldilocks is playing with Baby Bear. Mama Bear is watching and Papa Bear is sleeping. The mice cannot decide if they should stay or leave. **Fill in the missing letters so that each pair of words means the opposite.**

inside   __ __ __ side

__ __ ut   open

__ own   up

The Three Bears invited us in for a snack.
Look at what everyone is doing and read the words under the pictures. Circle the correct answer for each question.

asleep   awake

Are Papa and Mama doing the same thing?
Yes   No

stand

sit

Are Frankie and Floyd doing the same thing?
Yes   No

jump

hop

Are Goldilocks and Little Bear doing the same thing?
Yes   No

Who is deep in the woods of Fairy Tale Forest? Little Red Riding Hood. Help her through the forest. **Find the words in the box that mean the same as the picture words, and write them on the lines.**

huge	scared	tired	bad	small

little _____

afraid _____

big _____

sleepy _____

wicked _____

Grandma, what big teeth you have! Red Riding Hood had better be careful. Help her get away by filling in the missing words. **Read each word. Then fill in a word from the box that means the opposite.**

| off | far | under | closed | outside |

open _____

over _____

inside _____

on _____

near _____

Great job! Put your coin sticker in your money sack and jump ahead!

Antonyms and Synonyms

Frankie's Facts

Other words in a sentence can tell you if two words mean the **opposite** or the **same**.

We are back in the deep, dark forest. Hansel and Gretel look lost. **Use the words on the path to fill in the blanks in the sentences. Choose a word that means the same thing as the word in red.**

dark
cottage
wished
afraid
sounds

1. Hansel and Gretel were in the gloomy, _____ woods.

2. The two children were scared. They were _____ of witches.

3. Animals in the forest made lots of noises. Some of the _____ were near, and some were far.

4. Hansel and Gretel saw a sweet house, a charming _____.

5. Hansel wanted to go inside. Gretel _____ for the same thing.

Where did Hansel and Gretel go? Oh, well. I will look for treasure in this fireplace. Oh, no! The witch! Help us get out of here! **Fill in the missing words in the sentences below. Choose a word from the box that means the opposite of the word in red.**

| mean | away | free | shut | outside |

1. Hansel and Gretel went inside the house. Soon, they wanted to be back _____ !

2. The witch was nice at first. Then she got very _____ .

3. The children were trapped and could not get _____ .

4. Hansel and Gretel opened the fireplace door and then _____ it on the witch.

5. The children ran toward home and _____ from the witch's house.

Follow the path out of Fairy Tale Forest. **Read each word on the path.** If it is on a blue stone, write a word on the line that means the same. If it is on a yellow stone, write a word that means the opposite. Words to write are in the puddles near the path.

big
_____

sit
_____

thin
_____

glad
_____

pretty
_____

skinny
beautiful   stand
sad
large

awake
far jog

down
_____

near
_____

kind
_____

inside
_____

run
_____

asleep
_____

wicked
_____

up
nice
mean
outside

Words that sound the same but have different spellings and meanings are called **homophones**, or sound-alike words.

Now we are sailing to a castle to look for treasure. What will we find before we get there? Sound-alike words! **Look at the words in the word box and the words beneath the fish. Say each one out loud. Draw a line between the words that sound alike.**

| sea | sail | sun | hole | knot | tail |

son   see   not

sale   tale   whole

To get to the castle, you have to help the knight let the drawbridge down. **Draw a line from each word on one tower to the word on the other that sounds alike.**

hoarse

bear

be

night

nose

knows

bee

knight

bare

horse

Frankie's Facts

When words sound alike, you can get a clue for which word to use from its **meaning in a sentence**.

We took a wrong turn in the castle! I will see if my book can tell me where to go. Help me read part of the story. **Circle the correct word to finish each sentence.**

1. Watch out for the monster with the long **(tail)/tale**.

2. You do not want to **meet/meat** him up close.

3. He's someone you don't even want to **no/know**.

4. He **here's/hears** the smallest sound.

5. Run up the **stairs/stares** as fast as you can!

Whew! That monster was scary! Now we have to get through this path. **Read each word in the box. Then find a word on a bear that sounds the same. Draw a line to match the two.**

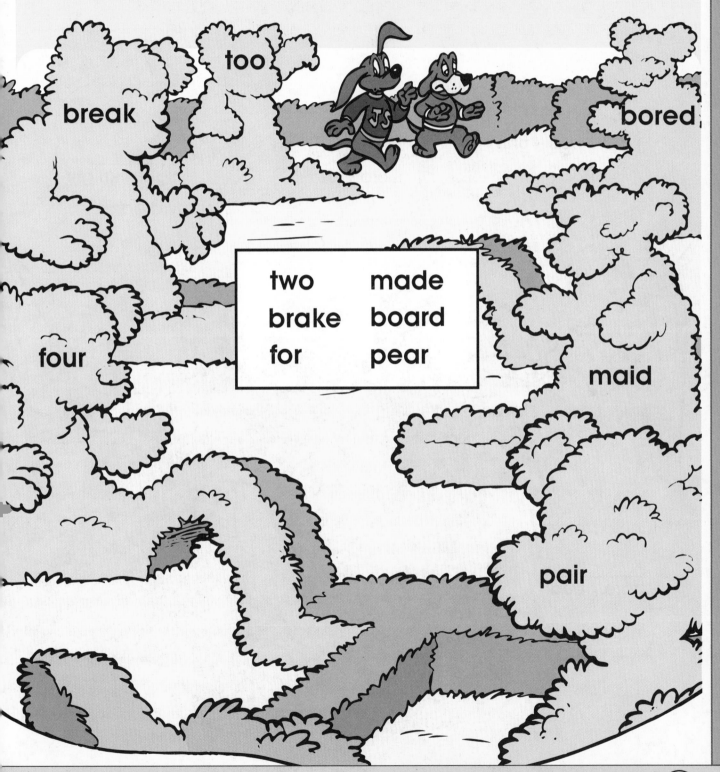

too

break

bored

two   made
brake board
for   pear

four

maid

pair

Let's listen closely! We may hear someone say where we can find some treasure. **Read each sentence. Fill in the correct word that fits the picture.**

You are the _____ for me.
won / one

Look for _____ crowns.
eight / ate

You are the _____ of my dreams.
night / knight

Look at the funny dancing _____.
bare / bear

Are you good with a bow and arrow? Try a little target practice.
Read the sentence on each target. Circle the word in the arrow that fits the sentence.

wear/where

What will you _____ to the castle?

red/read

I _____ a new book.

ate/eight

Floyd _____ a big cake.

pear/pair

I have a new _____ of shoes.

Frankie's Facts

When words sound alike, **spelling clues** can help you tell them apart.

Help! A dragon has come to the castle. There's only one way to stop it. **Read each clue. Circle a word on a flag that means the same thing and write it on the lines. Then write in the circled letters to answer the question below.**

pear/pair

red/rea_

weak/week

tale/tail

ate/eig_

Ⓦ _ _ _ _   1. seven days

_ _ ◯ _   2. a yellow fruit

_ _ _ _ ◯   3. the number after seven

_ _ ◯ _   4. a kind of story

◯ _ _ _   5. a bright color

What will keep the dragon out?   Ⓦ ◯ ◯ ◯ _ _ _ _

Maybe we can get a ride on this boat if we use these coins. Can you help? **Read the clues near each coin. Then write in the words that sound alike in the sets of coins below. Look for clues in the word box.**

two of a kind _____

a green or yellow fruit _____

it grows on your head _____

a rabbit _____

a kind of flower _____

lines _____

pear	pair
rows	rose
hare	hair

The fairy-tale characters want to play chess with us. Can you get everyone to the other side of the chessboard in two big jumps? **Read the words in each row. Then put an X on the homophone pair in each row. The last row has three pairs.**

	meat	a	blue	me	the
	pear	bored	the	tale	pour
	prince	hare	knight	a	one
	week	eye	green	sun	for
	night	tale	see	sea	sun

sun	meet	to	tale	hail	
pot	pair	won	I	meet	the end
hair	weak	strong	board	tail	
if	pair	weak	but	my	
by	knight	too	to	I	

Good game! Put your ring sticker on the Certificate of Completion and jump ahead!

Review (181)

Frankie's Facts

Words can tell us a lot about a picture. They can describe the things that are in it.

Uh-oh! Something on the bridge will not let us pass. Help us cross the bridge! **To get across, match the pictures with words in the word box. Write the correct number on each picture.**

| 1. leafy tree | 3. mean troll | 5. tall castle |
| 2. scary dragon | 4. cute goat | 6. deep river |

We got across! Now, the Three Little Pigs have invited us inside their house. Oh, no! The Big Bad Wolf is coming down the path. **Help the pigs keep him out by drawing a line from the words to the part of the picture they match.**

strong roof
shut door
red brick
hot pot

Does the elf have treasure in his sack? If you help him do his job, maybe he will tell you. **Match each picture to the sentence that talks about it. Draw lines between them.**

The Third Little Pig likes to read books.

Little Red Riding Hood's grandma gets a yummy cake.

Hansel and Gretel need a map of the woods.

The First Little Pig needs straw.

There are sticks for the Second Little Pig.

The prince is waiting for a saddle for his horse.

The gingerbread man just ran by!
He said the treasure was nearby and
he asked you to read his story.
**Draw a line from each sentence to the
picture it matches. Then number the
sentences to match the pictures.**

1.

☐ The gingerbread
man jumped out
of the oven.

3.

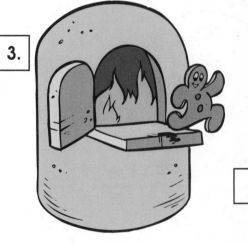

☐ A woman cut out a
gingerbread man.

☐ The gingerbread
man ran away.

☐ The woman put the
gingerbread man in
the oven.

4.

2.

Frankie's Facts

If you don't know a word in a story, **pictures and other words** can help you figure it out.

Maybe this frog can help us find the treasure. Read his story. **Use the pictures in the balloons to help you finish the sentences.**

| prince | princess | green | witch |

Once I was a handsome _____.

Then a mean _____ turned me into a frog.

My skin is all slimy and _____.

One kiss from a _____ could turn me back into a prince.

The princess is so beautiful. **Read her story and fill in the missing words.**

Once there was a _____ who was

very sad. She loved to read  _____ .

But she was lonely. She wished she could find a

 _____ who loved books, too.

She might fall in _____

with this prince.

You did it! Place your coin sticker in your money sack and jump ahead!

Reading and Writing (187)

Frankie's Facts

Answering questions about a sentence or a story can help you understand what you read.

The frog and the princess both need our help! What should we do? **Read the story below. Then answer the questions.**

The frog wants to turn back into a prince.

He needs to be kissed by a princess.

The princess would like to meet a prince who likes books.

She has a treasure for him.

Should we ask the frog if he likes books?

_____

If he says yes, what should we do?

_____

What can the princess do to help him?

_____

The frog is a prince again! A happy ending for all! **Look for the answers in the picture and write them on the lines.**

What is the princess's book about?

_____

How many crowns are on the wall?

_____

How do the prince and princess feel?

_____

Way to go! Put your coin sticker in your money sack and jump ahead!

Reading and Writing 189

When you go back to JumpStart School, you can take back some treasure—books! **Follow the path. Fill in the missing word on each fairy tale. Then the book is yours to take back. The missing words are in the word box.**

Goats Red Bears Pigs and Prince Man Island

START

The Gingerbread _____

The Three Billy _____ Gruff

Goldilocks and the Three _____

Little _____ Riding Hood

The Three Little _____

FINISH

The Frog _____

Fairy Tale _____

Hansel _____ Gretel

Congratulations! Put your belt sticker on your Certificate of Completion. You're ready to sail away!

Answer Key

PAGE 162 red: fast/slow, big/little, girl/boy, large/small; blue: run/jog, happy/glad

PAGE 163 large, big; pretty, beautiful; mad, angry; glad, happy; skinny, thin; small, little

PAGE 164 outside; shut; down

PAGE 165 Papa and Mama, no; Frankie and Floyd, no; Goldilocks and Little Bear, yes

PAGE 166 small, scared, huge, tired, bad

PAGE 167 closed, under, outside, off, far

PAGE 168 1. dark; 2. afraid; 3. sounds; 4. cottage; 5. wished

PAGE 169 1. outside; 2. mean; 3. free; 4. shut; 5. away

PAGES 170–171 large, stand, skinny, sad, beautiful, up, nice, outside, mean, awake, jog, far

PAGE 172 sea/see; sail/sale; sun/son; hole/whole; knot/not; tail/tale

PAGE 173 hoarse/horse; bear/bare; be/bee; night/knight; nose/knows

PAGE 174 1. tail; 2. meet; 3. know; 4. hears; 5. stairs

PAGE 175 two/too; made/maid; brake/break; board/bored; for/four; pear/pair

PAGE 176 one; eight; knight; bear

PAGE 177 wear; read; ate; pair

PAGE 178 1. week; 2. pear; 3. eight; 4. tale; 5. red; WATER

PAGE 179 pair, pear; hair, hare; rose, rows

PAGES 180–181 meat/meet; pear/pair; hare/hair; week/weak; night/knight; see/sea; too/to

PAGE 182 on tree — 1; on dragon — 2; on troll — 3; on goat — 4; on castle — 5; on river — 6

PAGE 183 draw lines to roof, door, bricks, pot

PAGE 184 draw lines from sentences to map, book, cake, straw, sticks, saddle

PAGE 185 draw lines from sentences to matching pictures: 1. A woman cut out a gingerbread man. 2. The woman put the ginger bread man in the oven. 3. The gingerbread man jumped out of the oven. 4. The ginger bread man ran away.

PAGE 186 prince; witch; green; princess

PAGE 187 princess; books; prince; love

PAGE 188 Possible answers include: Yes; Tell him we know a princess; Kiss him.

PAGE 189 A Frog Prince; eight; They are happy.

PAGES 190–191 The Gingerbread Man; The Three Billy Goats Gruff; The Three Little Pigs; The Frog Prince; Goldilocks and the Three Bears; Little Red Riding Hood; Fairy Tale Island; Hansel and Gretel

Welcome! I'm Frankie, and this is my best pal Floyd. We've got permission to dig for buried treasure out here in the JumpStart School playground. Come help us find it!

See these coin stickers? Every time you learn something new, you get one of these stickers to put in your money sack. When you finish a whole section, you'll get a big treasure sticker to put on the Certificate of Completion at the end of the book.

One more thing! When you see this picture, it means I'm there to help you. Just look for **Frankie's Facts**.

Are you ready? Let's go see what backyard adventures we can find!

Frankie's Facts

When you **count**, you say numbers in order. Numbers tell **how many** things.

I didn't find any coins or jewels here, but I found bones! The numbers tell how many bones I want to put in each pile. **Help me by drawing the right number of bones in each pile.**

I can't remember what I buried in each hole.
Draw a line from the holes to the matching number of things.

 **1**   

 **2**   

 **3**   

 **4**   

 **5**   

 **6**   

 **7**   

 **8**   

 **9**   

 **10**   

You did it! Put your coin sticker in your money sack and jump ahead to the next level!

Number Recognition

I guess birds of a feather *do* flock together! **Count all the orange birds and draw a line to the matching number on one of the seed bags. Then do the same for the other groups of birds.**

Which squirrel dug up each pile of nuts? Help me find out. **Count each pile and write the number of nuts on the line below. Then draw lines to match the numbers you wrote to the numbers the squirrels are holding.**

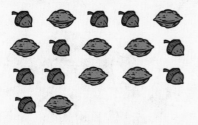

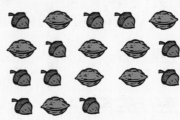

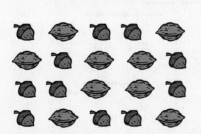  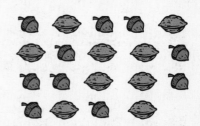

Frankie's Facts

You can count large numbers of things more easily if you **count by 10s**.

10, 20, 30, 40, 50,
60, 70, 80, 90, 100

We found more bones! **Help us find out how many we have. There are 10 bones in each pile. In each row, count the bones in the piles by 10s. Write the number on the line.**

The squirrels are going to share all these acorns. **Count by 10s and write the number of acorns in each row.**

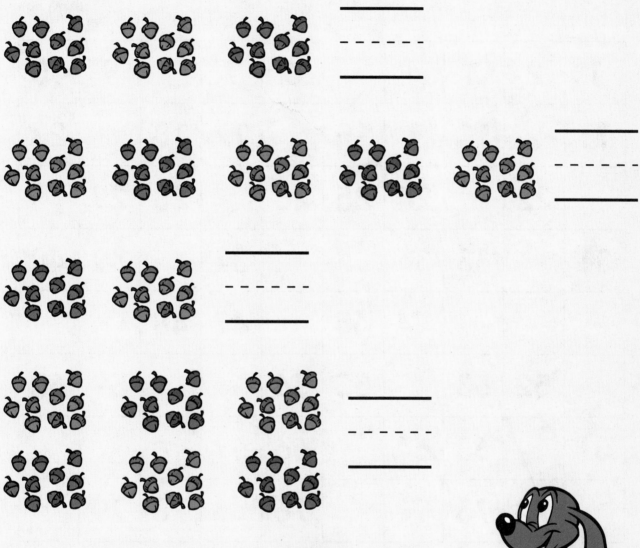

Let's count all the way to 100! **Fill in the missing numbers in order. Count out loud as you go.**

Start									
1	2	3	4		6	7		9	10
11		13		15		17	18		20
	22		24	25	26		28	29	
31		33	34			37		39	40
			44	45		47	48		
	52	53		55	56			59	60
61		63	64		66	67			
	72	73			76		78	79	
81			84	85			88		
91	92	93					98	99	100

Now circle all the numbers that end in 0.
Count down the column.
What are you counting by?

Looking for treasure is hard work. Let's monkey around on the monkey bars. **Help me climb down! Look at the numbers on each bar. Which number belongs in the middle? Write it on the line.**

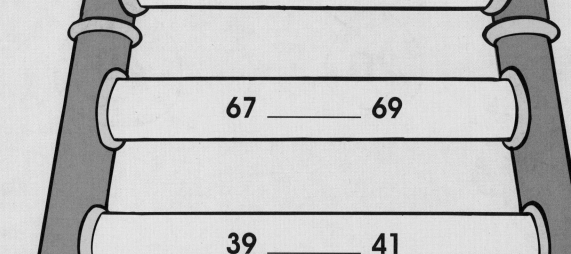

98 _____ 100

67 _____ 69

39 _____ 41

21 _____ 23

9 _____ 11   15 _____ 17

You're the tops! Put your coin sticker in your money sack and jump ahead!

Number Recognition (201)

Somebody was playing jacks on the playground. Let's put them away. Help us get each group of jacks into the right bag by drawing a line from each set to the bag with the matching number.

8

12

18

You really cleaned up! Place your gold bars sticker
on your Certificate of Completion and jump ahead!

Review (203)

Frankie's Facts

In a number **pattern**, numbers are arranged in a certain **order**.

1 2 3 1 2 3

10 20 30 40

Let's have some number fun on these swings. **Look at each row of numbers. Say each one out loud. Can you see the pattern? Write the number that comes next in the pattern.**

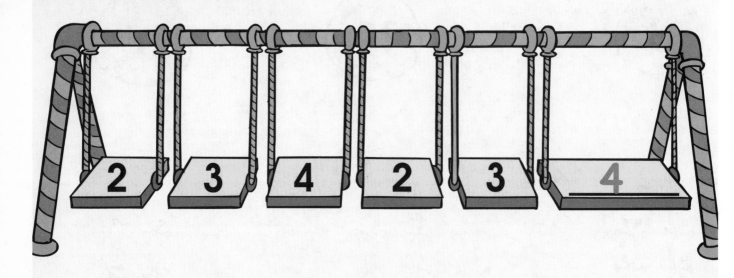

2   3   4   2   3   4

10   20   30   40   50   _____

1   2   3   4   5   _____

5   10   15   20   25   _____

Now let's slide down these number slides!
Look at the patterns. Can you write in the missing numbers?

Slide 1: 1, 2, ___, 4, 5, 6

Slide 2: 2, 4, 6, 8, ___, 12

Slide 3: 7, 8, 7, 8, 7, ___

Slide 4: 5, 10, ___, 20, 25, 30

You did it! Put your coin sticker in your money sack and jump ahead!

Frankie's Facts

+ means **plus**. We use it when we **add** numbers.

= means **equals**, or **is the same as**.

The **answer** is also the **sum**.

1 + 1 = 2

Well, we haven't found any treasure yet. Let's keep looking! **Look at all the balls on our playground. Can you help us add them up? Write the answers on each line.**

2   **+**   **2**   **=**   _____

4   **+**   **1**   **=**   _____

3   **+**   **3**   **=**   _____

2   **+**   **4**   **=**   _____

Is there treasure in this tree? No, but the birds have just laid some eggs in their nests. **Can you help me find the sum of the eggs in each row? Write the number on the line.**

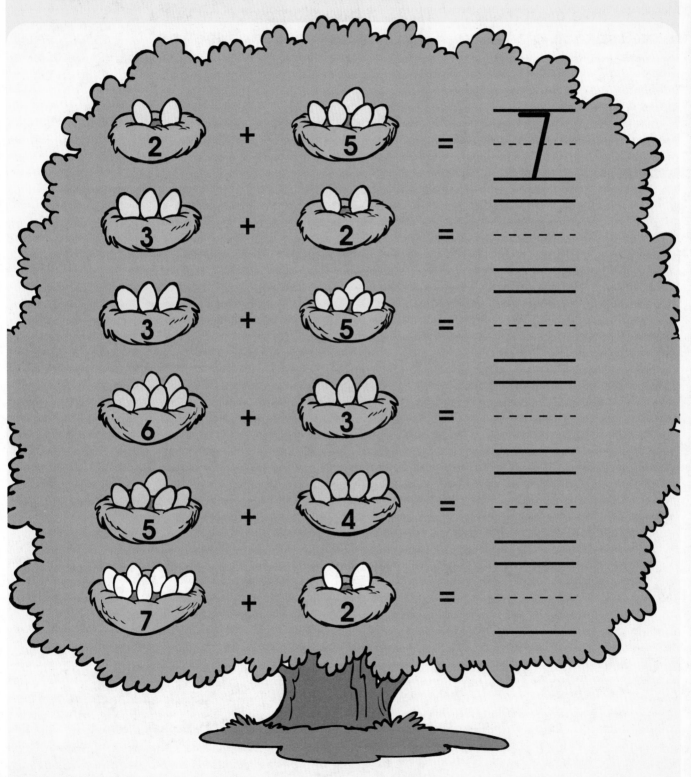

2 + 5 = 7

3 + 2 = ___

3 + 5 = ___

6 + 3 = ___

5 + 4 = ___

7 + 2 = ___

Frankie's Facts

— means **take away**. It shows we are **subtracting** one number from another. What you have left is the **remainder**.

$3 - 1 = 2$ ●○○ ● ○ – ○ ○ = ● ●

Peep, peep! The birds want to play a subtraction game with us. **Each row of nests is a subtraction problem. Write the remainder on the line.**

5 – 2 = 3

3 – 1 =

5 – 1 =

6 – 3 =

5 – 3 =

7 – 5 =

Frankie's Facts

Try counting **backwards** when you subtract!

$$9 - 6 = ?$$

Count backwards from **9** until you get to **6**.

8, 7, 6.

That's **three** numbers. The answer is **3**.

Birds, birds, everywhere! Some are flying away. **How many in each group will be left? Write the remainder on the line.**

$$9 \ - \ 7 \ = \ \underline{\hspace{2cm}}$$

$$6 \ - \ 5 \ = \ \underline{\hspace{2cm}}$$

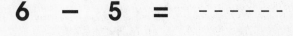

$$5 \ - \ 4 \ = \ \underline{\hspace{2cm}}$$

$$9 \ - \ 6 \ = \ \underline{\hspace{2cm}}$$

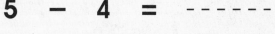

$$8 \ - \ 4 \ = \ \underline{\hspace{2cm}}$$

Good going! Put your coin sticker in your money sack and jump ahead!

Frankie's Facts

> and **<** mean **more than** or **less than**.

3 > 2 means that **3** is larger than **2**.

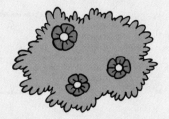 and look like alligators' mouths. The alligator **eats** the bigger number!

There's no treasure in this garden, but there are flowers. **In each picture, count the red and blue flowers. Write > or < to show which group is bigger.**

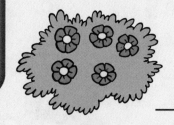

5   **>**   3

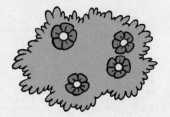

7   _____   5

4   _____   5

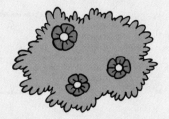

3   _____   6

We're tossing rings onto these sticks! My rings are red, and Floyd's are blue. **Count each stack of rings. Write those two numbers on the lines below each stick. Then write > or < to show which stick has more.**

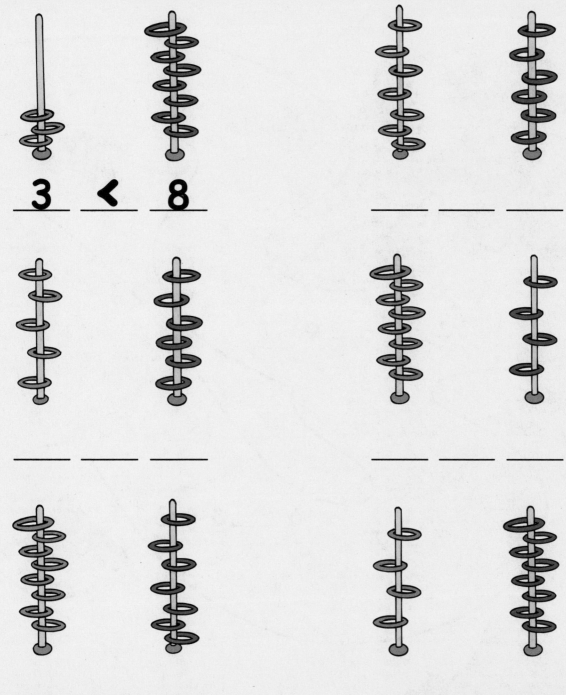

3 **<** **8**

___ ___ ___   ___ ___ ___

___ ___ ___   ___ ___ ___

___ ___ ___   ___ ___ ___

There may be some treasure down this path. Help me find my way! **Fill in a math symbol to complete each number sentence. Look in the box for reminders.**

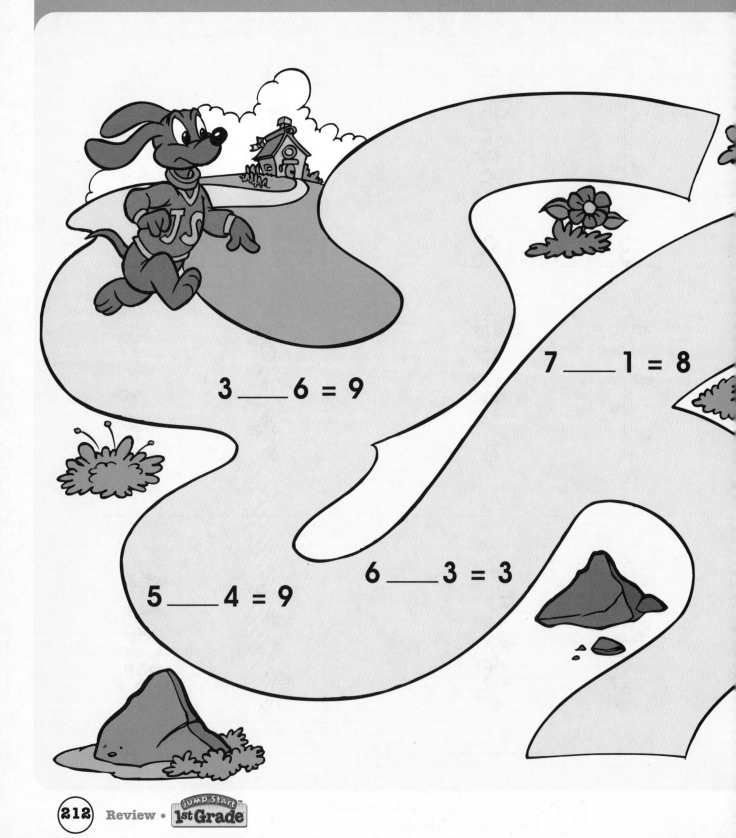

3 ___ 6 = 9

7 ___ 1 = 8

6 ___ 3 = 3

5 ___ 4 = 9

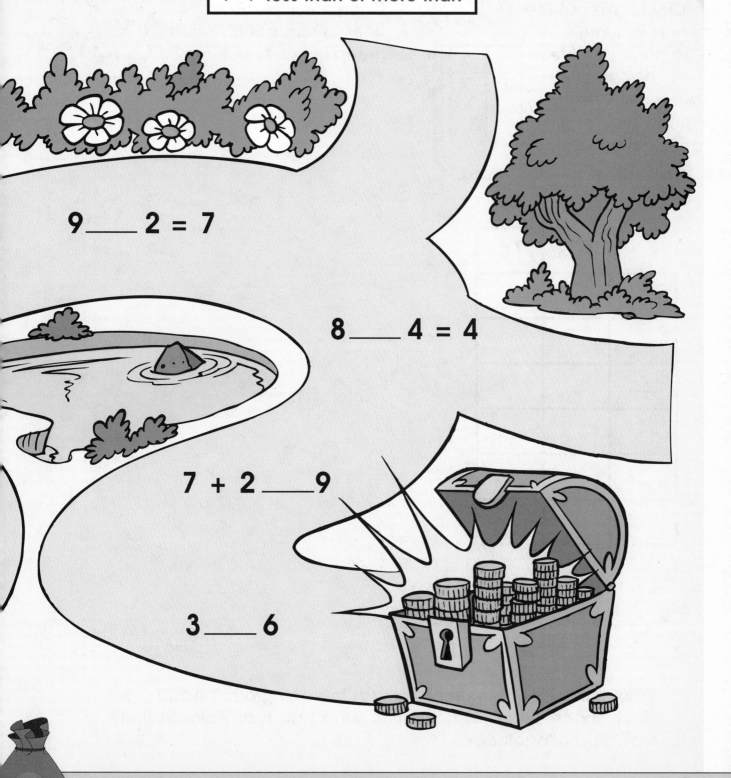

+ plus
− take away
= equals
>< less than or more than

9 ___ $2 = 7$

8 ___ $4 = 4$

$7 + 2$ ___ 9

3 ___ 6

You win! Place your treasure box sticker here and jump ahead!

Review 213

Frankie's Facts

The numbers **0** to **9** tell how many **1s**. We put them in the **1s column**.
The number **thirteen** has one **ten** and three **ones**. The three goes in the **ones column**.

10s	1s
1	3

I'm glad those don't look like rain clouds. Look how they float by in groups. **Can you write the correct number for each group in the 1s column?**

	10s	1s
🐑		
🐑		
☁️		
🐰		
❄️		
☁️		

What if there were ten more clouds in each group? Add 1s to each space in the 10s column to show how many clouds there would be altogether.

Do you think these kites can lead us to any more treasure?
How many are in each group? Write the correct numbers in the 10s and 1s columns.

	10s	1s
20 kites +	2	5
10 kites +		
30 kites +		
10 kites +		
10 kites +		
40 kites +		

You're number one! Put your coin sticker in your money sack and jump ahead!

Frankie's Facts

For numbers bigger than 9, you need to use the **10s column**.

10s	1s
1	3

Even treasure hunters have to eat! Let's have a cookout. Help us set up! **First, circle groups of 10 things. Count the leftover ones. Write each group of things on the lines and then write the correct numbers in the 10s and 1s columns.**

Things for Cookout	10s	1s
marshmallows	2	5
juice		
bread		
hot dogs		

So many ants came to our cookout! They even have team colors. How many are on each team? **Circle groups of 10 ants. Count the leftover ones. Write the correct numbers in the 10s and 1s columns.**

TEAM	10s	1s
Blue team		
Red team		
Orange team		
Green team		
Purple team		

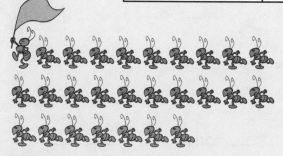

That was a good cookout. Now let's look for more treasure and leave no stone unturned. In each row of stones, how many 10s are there? How many 1s?

Circle each group of tens and count the leftover ones. Write your answers on the lines. Then write the total amount of stones in each group.

_____ tens + _____ ones = _____

_____ tens + _____ ones = _____

_____ tens + _____ ones = _____

_____ tens + _____ ones = _____

Uh-oh! It's getting windy. Look at all the leaves blowing off the trees. How many 10s and 1s are there in each group? **Circle the groups of 10s and count the leftover 1s. Then fill in the numbers in the columns below.**

	10s	1s
🍃		
🍂		
🍃		
🌿		

You're a two-column wonder! Put your coin sticker in your money sack and jump ahead!

Level 2

Frankie's Facts

You write **99** with
9 in the **10s** column and
9 in the **1s** column.
Next comes **100**.
The **1** is in the **100s** column.

100s	10s	1s
	9	9
1	0	0

It's almost time to go—let's count our treasure! **Read the questions below. Write the answers on the lines.**

100　　　**10**　　　**1**

If we dug up:

193 coins, how many would we have?

100s? 　　　 10s? 　　　 1s?

227 coins, how many would we have?

100s? 　　　 10s? 　　　 1s?

406 coins, how many would we have?

100s? 　　　 10s? _____ 1s? _____

360 coins, how many would we have?

100s? _____ 10s? _____ 1s? _____

Will you help me buy the bricks we need to make our playhouse?
First, look at the number of bricks we might need. Then write the answers on the lines.

432 How many 100s? _____ 10s? _____ 1s? _____

165 How many 100s? _____ 10s? _____ 1s? _____

340 How many 100s? _____ 10s? _____ 1s? _____

572 How many 100s? _____ 10s? _____ 1s? _____

109 How many 100s? _____ 10s? _____ 1s? _____

Wow! Put your coin sticker in your money sack and jump ahead!

What a fun day on the playground. Will you help us sail away by carrying some coins to the ship? **The numbers on each sack show how many coins are inside. Write the correct number of 100s, 10s, and 1s on the lines. Look at the box for a reminder of place value.**

80

_____ _____ _____

158

_____ _____ _____

400

393

_____ _____ _____

_____ _____ _____

You're a treasure! Place your genie lamp
sticker on your Certificate of Completion.

Review   223

Answer Key

PAGE 194   draw 2 bones, 3 bones, 4 bones, 5 bones, 6 bones, 7 bones, 8 bones, 9 bones, 10 bones

PAGE 195   connect 1/button, 2/thimbles, 3/acorns, 4/apples, 5/ bowling balls, 6 pins, 7/pencils, 8/cars, 9/bubbles, 10/popcorns

PAGE 196   connect orange birds/11, blue birds/15, green birds/13, red birds/12, yellow birds/14

PAGE 197   write and connect 17, 18, 20, 16, 19

PAGE 198   write 10, 20, 30, 40, 50, 60, 70, 80

PAGE 199   write 30, 50, 20, 60

PAGE 200   write 5, 8, 12, 14, 16, 19, 21, 23, 27, 30, 32, 35, 36, 38, 41, 42, 43, 46, 49, 50, 51, 54, 57, 58, 62, 65, 68, 69, 70, 71, 74, 75, 77, 80, 82, 83, 86, 87, 89, 90, 94, 95, 96, 97; circle 10, 20, 30, 40, 50, 60, 70, 80, 90, 100; by 10s

PAGE 201   write 99, 68, 40, 22, 10, 16

PAGES 202–203   connect 20/orange jacks, 40/blue jacks, 8/red jacks, 12/yellow jacks, 18/green jacks

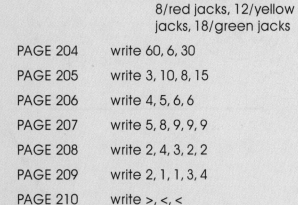

PAGE 204   write 60, 6, 30

PAGE 205   write 3, 10, 8, 15

PAGE 206   write 4, 5, 6, 6

PAGE 207   write 5, 8, 9, 9, 9

PAGE 208   write 2, 4, 3, 2, 2

PAGE 209   write 2, 1, 1, 3, 4

PAGE 210   write >, <, <

PAGE 211   write 7 > 6, 5 < 6, 8 > 4, 8 > 7, 4 < 8

PAGES 212–213   write +, +, -, +, -, -, =, <

PAGE 214   write 3, 6, 4, 5, 7, 9; write 1 in 10s column six times

PAGE 215   write 1/6, 3/2, 1/4, 1/8, 4/7

PAGE 216   circle groups of 10 things; (order may vary) write juice/1/2, rolls/1/1, hot dogs/1/4

PAGE 217   circle groups of 10 ants; write 3/5, 2/4, 2/7, 3/0, 4/2

PAGE 218   circle groups of 10; write 4/2/42, 1/4/14, 1/6/16, 2/5/25

PAGE 219   circle groups of 10; write 2/6, 4/3, 3/7, 5/1

PAGE 220   write 1/9/3, 2/2/7, 4/0/6, 3/6/0

PAGE 221   write 4/3/2, 1/6/5, 3/4/0, 5/7/2, 1/0/9

PAGES 222–223   write 0/4/0, 2/0/3, 2/1/1, 0/8/6, 0/6/7, 0/8/0, 1/5/8, 4/0/0, 3/9/3

Welcome! I'm Frankie, and this is my best pal, Floyd. We are going on an adventure in my backyard. Who knows what we will find? Why don't you come along!

See these coins? Each time you learn something new, you will get a coin sticker to put in your money sack. When you finish a whole section, you will get a big treasure sticker to put on your Certificate of Completion at the end of the book.

Take a look at this picture of me.
When you see it in the book,
it means I'm there to help you.
Just look for **Frankie's Facts**.

Come join us!
Let's go see
what backyard
adventures we
can find!

Frankie's Facts

Adding means finding out how many things there are altogether. When you **add** numbers, you get their **sum**.

Wow! Look at all these ants. How many do you think there are?

Count each group of ants and write the correct number under each picture. Then add both groups together. Write the sum on the line at the right.

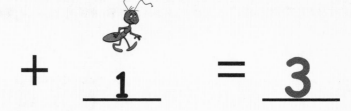

__2__ + __1__ = __3__

___ + ___ = ___

___ + ___ = ___

___ + ___ = ___

Bunnies, bunnies, bunnies! How many are in the bunny hole?

Write the numbers under
each group of bunnies.
Then count how many
bunnies there are in
each row and
write the sum.

 + =

_____   _____   _____

_____   _____   _____

 + =

_____   _____   _____

 +  =

_____   _____   _____

**Way to go! Put your coin sticker in the money
sack. Now jump ahead to the next level.**

Frankie's Facts

You can count things out loud to find the answer. The answer is also called the **sum**.

🐰 + 🐰 = 🐰🐰

1 + 1 = 2

There's a bunny hop going on in my backyard. Will you help us add up these bunnies?

How many bunnies are there altogether in each row?

🐰🐰 **+** 🐰 **=** _____

🐰🐰 **+** 🐰🐰 **=** _____

🐰🐰🐰 **+** 🐰 **=** _____

🐰🐰🐰🐰 **+** 🐰 **=** _____

🐰🐰🐰🐰🐰 **+** 🐰🐰 **=** _____

Can you count all the bunnies on the page? Write how many there are. _____

Look what I found in the bunny hole!

Which is the way out? Help me add up all the bunnies.

5 + 2 = _____   3 + 1 = _____   4 + 9 = _____

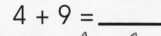

1 + 6 = _____   3 + 3 = _____   5 + 1 = _____

Circle the largest group of bunnies.

Frankie's Facts

You can also add numbers **up and down**. It is the same as adding them side to side.

$$3 + 2 = \underline{\qquad}$$

$$\begin{array}{r} 3 \\ + 2 \\ \hline \end{array}$$

Look! The tree in my backyard has four strong branches. Each one has two nests with baby birds.

Help me add the birds on each branch.

$$\begin{array}{r} 2 \\ + 3 \\ \hline \end{array}$$

$$\begin{array}{r} 2 \\ + 2 \\ \hline \end{array}$$

$$\begin{array}{r} 3 \\ + 5 \\ \hline \end{array}$$

$$\begin{array}{r} 5 \\ + 2 \\ \hline \end{array}$$

Floyd and I love dog bones! We hid them all over the yard.

Can you help us add up all our bones?

4
+ 2
—
6

3
+ 1
—

5
+ 3
—

6
+ 3
—

3
+ 3
—

Great job! Put your coin sticker in the money sack and jump ahead to the next level!

Addition (231)

Frankie's Facts

To add numbers with 10s and 1s, first you add the **1s column** on the **right**. Then you add the **10s column** on the **left**.

$$
\begin{array}{r}
12 \\
+\ 1 \\
\hline
13
\end{array}
$$

These bugs are fun to watch. There are so many!

Help us add all these numbers so we can count the bugs.

$$
\begin{array}{r}
10 \\
+\ 1 \\
\hline
11
\end{array}
\qquad
\begin{array}{r}
12 \\
+\ 5 \\
\hline
\end{array}
\qquad
\begin{array}{r}
14 \\
+\ 12 \\
\hline
\end{array}
\qquad
\begin{array}{r}
11 \\
+\ 5 \\
\hline
\end{array}
$$

$$
\begin{array}{r}
13 \\
+\ 22 \\
\hline
\end{array}
\qquad
\begin{array}{r}
16 \\
+\ 13 \\
\hline
\end{array}
\qquad
\begin{array}{r}
24 \\
+\ 25 \\
\hline
\end{array}
\qquad
\begin{array}{r}
10 \\
+\ 10 \\
\hline
\end{array}
$$

Hip, hip, hooray! The mice are having a parade.

Add these numbers to join the fun.

12	11	12	13
+ 4	+ 5	+ 7	+ 12

———— ———— ———— ————

10	16	22
+ 15	+ 13	+ 16

———— ———— ————

What is the highest sum? _____

What is the lowest sum? _____

Fantastic! Put your coin sticker in the money sack and jump ahead to see what you've learned.

Addition 233

We love to jump and roll around in the leaves! How many do you think will fall around us?

Count the leaves in each group and write the sum on the line.

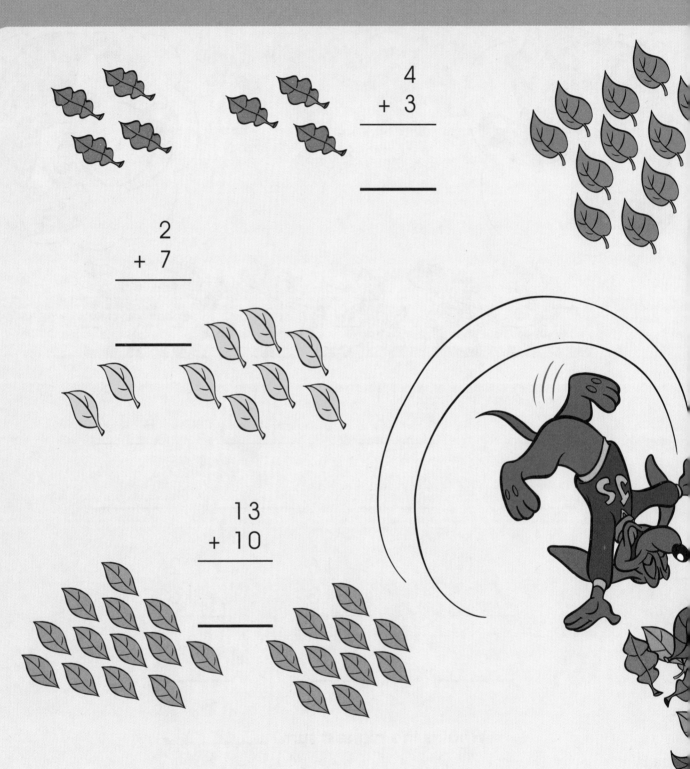

$$\begin{array}{r} 4 \\ + 3 \\ \hline \end{array}$$

$$\begin{array}{r} 2 \\ + 7 \\ \hline \end{array}$$

$$\begin{array}{r} 13 \\ + 10 \\ \hline \end{array}$$

$$12 + 5$$

$$14 + 11$$

$$12 + 16$$

Excellent! Place your ring sticker on
the Certificate of Completion and jump ahead.

Review 235

Frankie's Facts

When you **subtract**, you take something away.

Look at all these frogs! Some want to go swimming in the pond.

In each group, count the number of frogs. Make an X on each frog that is jumping away. How many frogs are left? Write the number on the line.

_____

_____

_____

_____

If there were 6 frogs in a group and 0 went swimming, how many would be left?

_____

There sure are a lot of flowers here. Let's bring some back for our teacher.

Count the flowers in each group. Look at how many we're picking. How many flowers will be left?

 —  = _____

 —  = _____

 —  = _____

 —  = _____

 —  = _____

Way to go! Put your coin sticker in the money sack. Now jump ahead to the next level.

Frankie's Facts

You can subtract numbers the same way you subtracted things. What's left is called the **difference**.

2 – 1 = 1

Floyd was going to help me count how many bees were left, but he buzzed off.

Count the total number of bees in each hive. Now subtract the bees that are leaving the hive. Write the difference on the line.

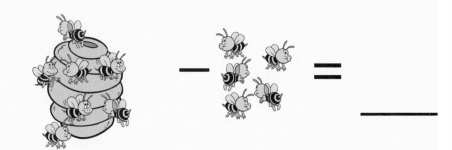

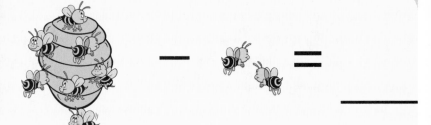

Floyd and I are worm watching. **Count the worms in each group. Make X's on the worms that are inching away. Write how many worms are left.**

9 – 2 = _____   5 – 2 = _____   6 – 2 = _____

4 – 3 = _____   3 – 2 = _____   9 – 7 = _____

Let's help the spider finish her web.

Find the difference for each equation. Write your answers on the lines next to the dots. Then connect the rest of the dots to finish the web.

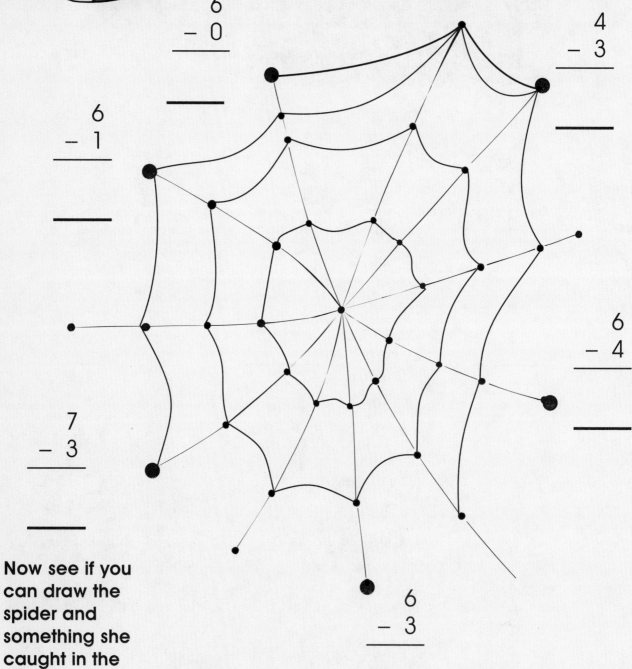

$$\begin{array}{r} 6 \\ -\ 0 \\ \hline \end{array}$$

$$\begin{array}{r} 4 \\ -\ 3 \\ \hline \end{array}$$

$$\begin{array}{r} 6 \\ -\ 1 \\ \hline \end{array}$$

$$\begin{array}{r} 6 \\ -\ 4 \\ \hline \end{array}$$

$$\begin{array}{r} 7 \\ -\ 3 \\ \hline \end{array}$$

$$\begin{array}{r} 6 \\ -\ 3 \\ \hline \end{array}$$

Now see if you can draw the spider and something she caught in the web.

The birds are hungry, but the worms are fast.

Do the subtraction to help us find out how many worms wriggled away.

9
− 4
_____

5
− 4
_____

7
− 1
_____

8
− 5
_____

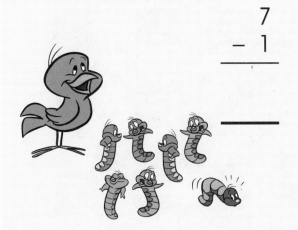

7
− 6
_____

Good work! Put your coin sticker in the money sack and jump ahead to the next level.

Frankie's Facts

My pal Floyd and I are having a snack of 16 bones.

Count all the bones. Then do the subtraction below to find the differences.

To subtract numbers with 10s and 1s, first you subtract the **1s column** on the **right**. Then you subtract the **10s column** on the **left**. (You don't have to write a zero if there's nothing left in the 10s column.)

```
  16
-  3
____


  16
-  5
____
```

```
  16        16        16        16
-  6      - 10      - 12      - 15
____      ____      ____      ____
```

How many bones would we have left if we gave away 7? 8? 9? 13?

There are 18 snails in the backyard. Every hour some crawl away.

How many snails are still out in the backyard each hour?

12 o'clock
$$\begin{array}{r} 18 \\ -\ \ 3 \\ \hline \end{array}$$

1 o'clock
$$\begin{array}{r} 18 \\ -\ \ 5 \\ \hline \end{array}$$

2 o'clock
$$\begin{array}{r} 18 \\ -\ \ 6 \\ \hline \end{array}$$

3 o'clock
$$\begin{array}{r} 18 \\ -\ 10 \\ \hline \end{array}$$

4 o'clock
$$\begin{array}{r} 18 \\ -\ 12 \\ \hline \end{array}$$

5 o'clock
$$\begin{array}{r} 18 \\ -\ 15 \\ \hline \end{array}$$

What time are most of the snails in the backyard? _____

Way to go! Put your coin sticker in the money sack and jump ahead to see what you've learned.

Subtraction 243

Let's go apple picking. **Solve** the subtraction problems to help us put the apples in our baskets.

$$\begin{array}{r} 20 \\ -\ 10 \\ \hline \end{array}$$

$$\begin{array}{r} 24 \\ -\ 13 \\ \hline \end{array}$$

Can you solve these problems, too?

$$\begin{array}{r} 23 \\ -\ 12 \\ \hline \end{array} \qquad \begin{array}{r} 25 \\ -\ 2 \\ \hline \end{array} \qquad \begin{array}{r} 12 \\ -\ 3 \\ \hline \end{array} \qquad \begin{array}{r} 16 \\ -\ 4 \\ \hline \end{array} \qquad \begin{array}{r} 13 \\ -\ 2 \\ \hline \end{array}$$

18
− 7

16
− 5

19
− 9

25
− 14

Great job! Put your urn sticker on the
Certificate of Completion and jump ahead.

Review (245)

Frankie's Facts

Measuring can tell you the size of something. You can also see how things are alike or different by comparing measurements.

I've met some new friends on my backyard adventure.

How do we compare in size? Read the questions and look at the pictures. Then draw circles around the answers.

Who is smaller?

Who is bigger?

Who is longer?

Who is heavier?

Who is shorter?

On a separate piece of paper, draw something that is smaller than you.

It's harvest time! Let's pick things from our garden. **The word under each pair tells you which one I want. Circle the picture that matches the word.**

longer

bigger

heavier

taller

larger

shorter

On a separate piece of paper, draw the biggest and smallest food you can think of.

Wonderful! Put your coin sticker in the money sack and jump ahead to the next level.

Measurement

Frankie's Facts

A **ruler** measures how long, how tall, or how high. A **scale** shows how heavy. A **measuring cup** shows how much space something takes up. A **thermometer** shows how hot or cold.

Floyd and I are playing leapfrog. Which measuring tool would you use to measure our jumps? You're right if you guessed a ruler!

Circle the measuring tool you would use to do these other things.

bake a cake				

draw a line				

see how you feel				

see how much something weighs				

Let's measure together.

Look at the measuring tools in each box. Then look at the pictures in the row next to it. Cross out the one you would be least likely to measure with that tool.

Floyd and I have invited some dog friends over.

Put the dogs in order from shortest to tallest, using the numbers 1 (shortest) to 5 (tallest).

_____   _____   _____   1   _____

Floyd and I want to ride the seesaw in my backyard. Which one of us do you think will go up? Who will go down?

Circle the animal below who will make the seesaw go down.

Write what you think would happen if two animals that weighed the same got on a seesaw.

_____

_____

_____

_____

Fantastic! Put your coin sticker in the money sack and jump ahead to the next level.

Measurement (251)

Frankie's Facts

If you don't have a measuring tool, you can **estimate** size by using other things. Hold up your little finger. How big is it compared to the animals on this page?

I am going to see how long all my little friends are. But I don't have a ruler. Maybe I will use this little bone. It is one inch long.

Circle the friends that are the same size as this one-inch bone.

It looks like some friends are heading for my doghouse. I will use my foot to measure how big their feet are.

Draw circles around all the footprints that are bigger than my foot. Make X's on the footprints that are smaller than my foot. Then follow each path to see who is waiting for me. Draw a circle around the friend with the smallest feet.

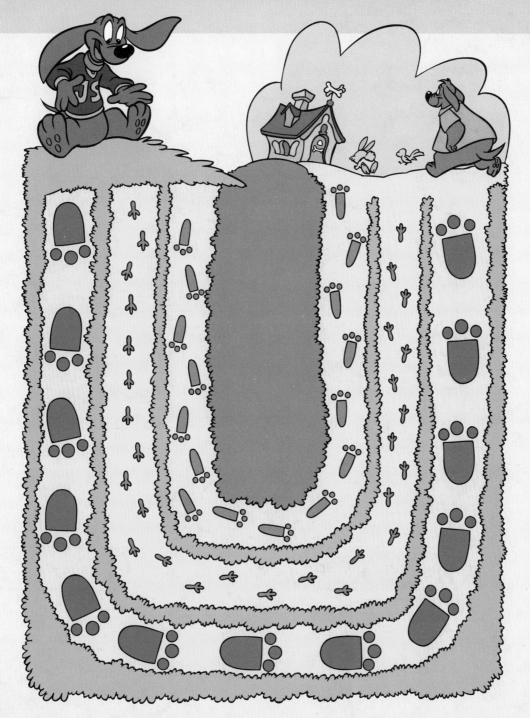

How many footprints are on this page?

Way to go! Put your coin sticker in the money sack and jump ahead to see what you've learned.

Measurement **253**

How tall?

How hot?

How much?

How long?

How heavy?

Measuring Cup

Ruler

We've had so many adventures today! Now let's see how everything around me measures up. **Read the words at the bottom of the page. Draw lines from the pictures to the tools that would help you answer the questions near the things in the picture.**

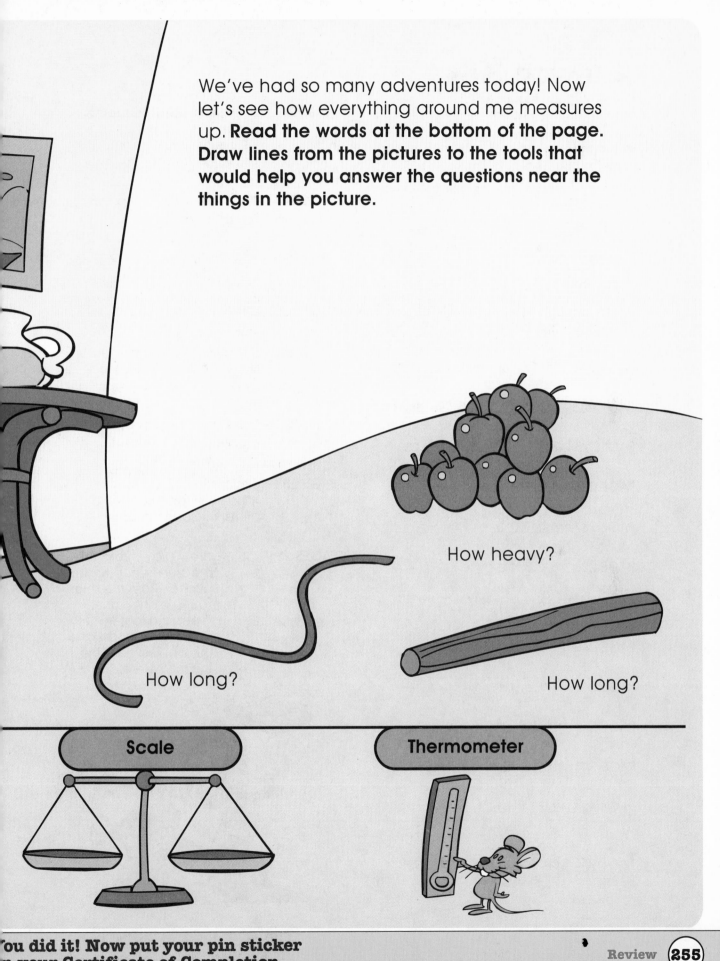

How heavy?

How long?

How long?

Scale

Thermometer

You did it! Now put your pin sticker on your Certificate of Completion.

Review 255

Answer Key

PAGE 226 2+1=3; 2+2=4; 4+1=5; 5+2=7

PAGE 227 2+3=5; 4+4=8; 6+2=8; 3+6=9

PAGE 228 3, 4, 4, 5, 7; 23

PAGE 229 7, 7, 4, 6, 13, 6; circle the group of 9

PAGE 230 5, 4, 8, 7

PAGE 231 6, 4, 8, 9, 6

PAGE 232 11, 17, 26, 16; 35, 29, 49, 20

PAGE 233 16, 16, 19, 25, 25, 29, 38; 38, 16

PAGES 234–235 7, 9, 23, 17, 25, 28

PAGE 236 3, 5, 1, 4, 2; 6

PAGE 237 4, 3, 1, 0, 5

PAGE 238 5, 2, 3, 4

PAGE 239 7, 3, 4, 1, 1, 2

PAGE 240 1, 2, 3, 4, 5, 6

PAGE 241 5, 1, 6, 3, 1

PAGE 242 13, 11, 10, 6, 4, 1; 9, 8, 7, 3

PAGE 243 15, 13, 12, 8, 6, 3; 12 o'clock

PAGES 244–245 10, 11, 11, 11, 10, 11; 11, 23, 9, 12, 11

PAGE 246 circle: bug, Frankie, snake, other dog, bird; pictures will vary

PAGE 247 circle: left carrot, left tomato, right melon, right mushroom, left squash, bottom wheat; drawings will vary

PAGE 248 circle: measuring cup, ruler, thermometer, scale

PAGE 249 cross out: milk, green circle, dress, cereal box

PAGE 250 2, 5, 3, 1, 4

PAGE 251 circle: Frankie, Floyd, mouse, larger dog, larger snake; seesaw would balance

PAGE 252 circle: inchworm, bee, caterpillar

PAGE 253 circle: the big dog prints; draw X's on the rabbit and bird prints; circle the bird; 58

PAGES 254–255 draw a line: from the measuring cup to the pitcher; from the ruler to the plant, bone, rope, and log; from the scale to the shoe and the apples; from the thermometer to the cup

Hi! I'm Frankie, and this is my best pal Floyd. He's the hall monitor at the JumpStart school. He's great to have around when it's time for any kind of adventure. Let's explore our school!

See these coin stickers? Every time you learn something new, you get one of these stickers to put in your money sack. When you finish a whole section, you'll get a big treasure sticker to put on your Certificate of Completion at the end of the book.

One more thing! When you see this picture of me, it means I'm there to help you. Just look for **Frankie's Facts**.

OK? Let's get started.

Frankie's Facts

The **numbers** on a watch or a clock show what time it is. The little hand is called the **hour hand**. It tells what hour it is.

It is **8 o'clock**.

It's about time I got my own watch! Now I won't be late for school. Can you help me write the numbers on my watch?
Trace them in order, from 1 to 12.

I'm going to set these clocks. Help me make sure I have the times right.

Draw a line from each clock to the time that matches. Then color in each clock.

10:00

2:00

5:00

3:00

7:00

6:00

You did it! Put your coin sticker on your money sack and jump ahead to the next level!

Time **259**

Frankie's Facts

You can also write the time like this: **2:00**. That means the same as **2 o'clock**.

Floyd is handing out hall passes. **Read the time on each pass. Draw an hour hand on each clock to show that time.**

8:00

9:00

1:00

11:00

12:00

4:00

Look! Ms. Nobel, the teacher, has written a schedule on the board, but these clocks don't have hands!
Draw a big hand and a little hand on each clock to show the right time.

7:00	get up
8:00	start school
10:00	go to recess
12:00	eat lunch
1:00	finish lunch
3:00	go home

get up

start school

go to recess

eat lunch

finish lunch

go home

What time do you get up in the morning?

I'm helping Chef Gumbo the Octopus make lunch. We have lots to do.
Look at the hands on each clock.
Then write the time on the line below.

START SOUP

8 o'clock

BAKE CUPCAKES

_____ o'clock

CUT UP VEGETABLES

_____ o'clock

MAKE SANDWICHES

_____ o'clock

SERVE LUNCH

_____ o'clock

CLEAN UP

_____ o'clock

The clocks on these doors tell us what time we should be in each room.

Write the time in two different ways on each door. Color the door we go to first, red. Color the door we go to next, yellow. Color the third door green. Color the last door blue.

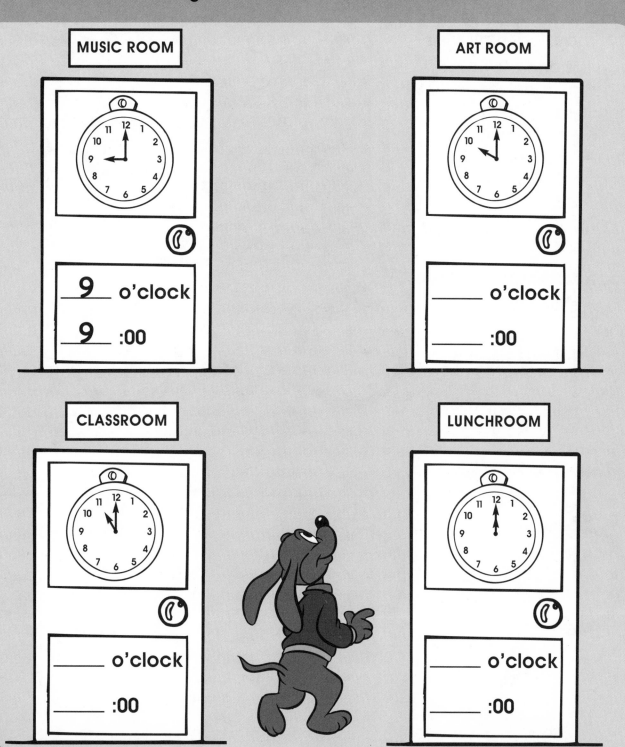

MUSIC ROOM

9 o'clock

9 :00

ART ROOM

_____ o'clock

_____ :00

CLASSROOM

_____ o'clock

_____ :00

LUNCHROOM

_____ o'clock

_____ :00

Right on time! Put your coin sticker on your money sack and jump ahead to the next level!

Frankie's Facts

From one o'clock to two o'clock is one hour.

one hour = 60 minutes
a half hour = 30 minutes

When it is **one o'clock**, the big hand points to the **12**. When it is **one-thirty**, the big hand moves half an hour and points to the **6**.

The clock near each oven tells us what time to take out the food. **Read each clock and write the time on the line.**

8:30 _____   _____   _____

_____   _____   _____

264 Time • 1st Grade

I was so excited for school, I didn't sleep much last night. Now I need a nap! Floyd set these alarm clocks to wake me up.

Read each clock with the time shown in numbers. Then draw in hands on the alarm clock to show the same time.

Great job! Put your coin sticker on your money sack and jump ahead!

Can you help Floyd and me find our way through this clock maze?

Follow the path where the times are in order. Draw a line along the path until you reach the end.

FINISH

Time is on your side! Place your clock sticker on the Certificate of Completion. Then jump ahead!

Review 267

Frankie's Facts

Each coin is worth a different amount.

penny = 1¢

nickel = 5¢

dime = 10¢

quarter = 25¢

¢ means **cents**. One penny equals one cent.

The JumpStart school kitchen needs more food. Floyd and I are going to the store to buy some. Let's see how much money I have.
Trace the numbers under each coin.

penny	**nickel**	**dime**	**quarter**
1¢	5¢	10¢	25¢

Now look at a *real* penny, nickel, dime, and quarter. Can you find the words "penny," "nickel," "dime," and "quarter" on them?

Floyd and I made it to the store. Where should we start?
Draw lines from our coins to the food we could buy with them.

5¢ 1¢ 5¢ 5¢ 1¢ 1¢

Excellent! Put your coin sticker on your money sack and jump ahead to the next level!

Money   269

Frankie's Facts

Groups of coins can add up to the same number of cents.

5 pennies + 1 nickel = 1 dime

Can you help Floyd figure out how many pennies equal the amount on the signs?
Look at the sign on each shelf. Then draw one penny on each can to add up to that amount.

1¢

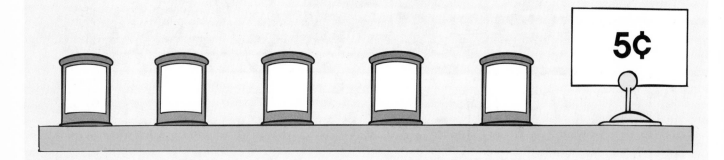

5¢

10¢

Which shelf equals one nickel? Color in the sign green.
Which shelf equals one dime? Color in the sign blue.

Each of these cheeses costs 10¢ a slice. Can you help Floyd figure out the coins he needs to buy each slice of cheese? **Look at how many coins he has for each slice of cheese. Then draw the coins under the cheeses. Choose from the coins in the box.**

Floyd has **2** coins:	Floyd has **10** coins:	Floyd has **1** coin:	Floyd has **6** coins:
5¢ 5¢			

Mmm! Watermelon! This slice costs 10¢.
**Count the coins in each group. If they
equal 10¢, draw a line to connect them
to the watermelon.**

We've been at the store so long, Floyd is getting a little confused!

Can you help him remember how much a nickel and a dime are worth? In each box, draw how many pennies each coin equals.

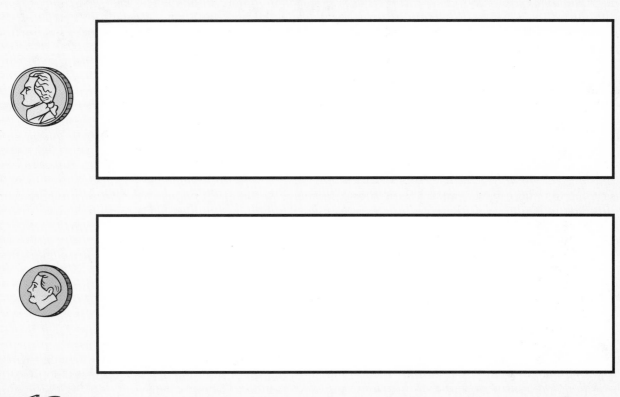

Great! Put your coin sticker on your money sack and jump ahead to the next level!

Money 273

Frankie's Facts

Quarters are worth **25¢**. Two dimes and a nickel equal one quarter.

 + + =

Floyd and I are ready to pay. How much does each item cost? **Count up the coins next to it and write the amount next to the picture.**

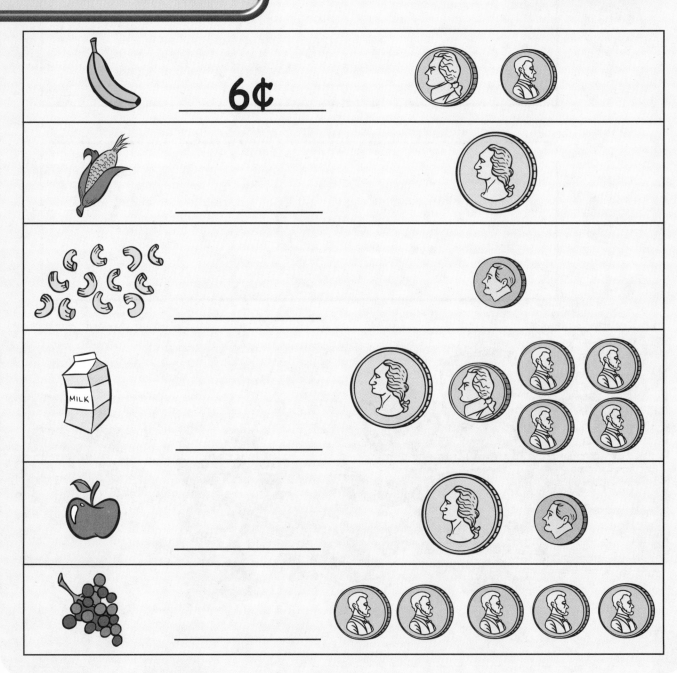

6¢

Floyd and I have change left over from shopping. We're putting our coins back in our piggy banks.
Add up how much money we put in each piggy bank.

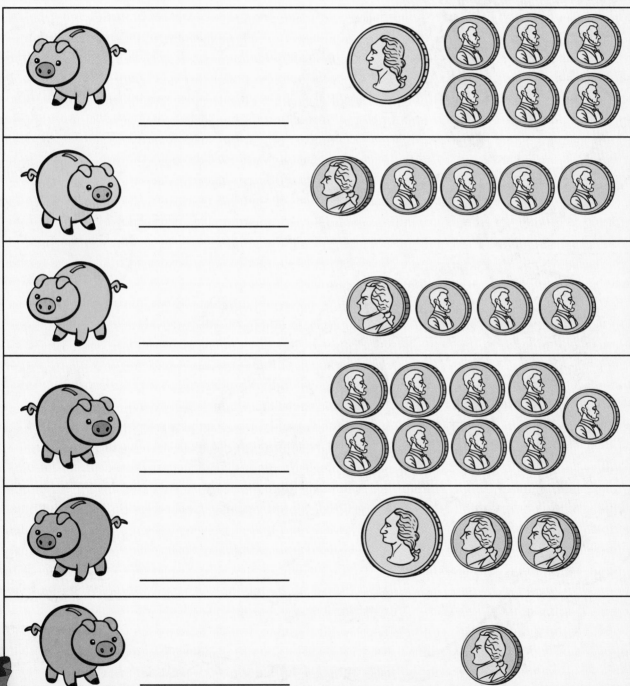

Fantastic! Put your coin sticker on your money sack and jump ahead!

Money 275

Look at this money maze! To get to the end, follow the path where each group of coins adds up to more than the one before.

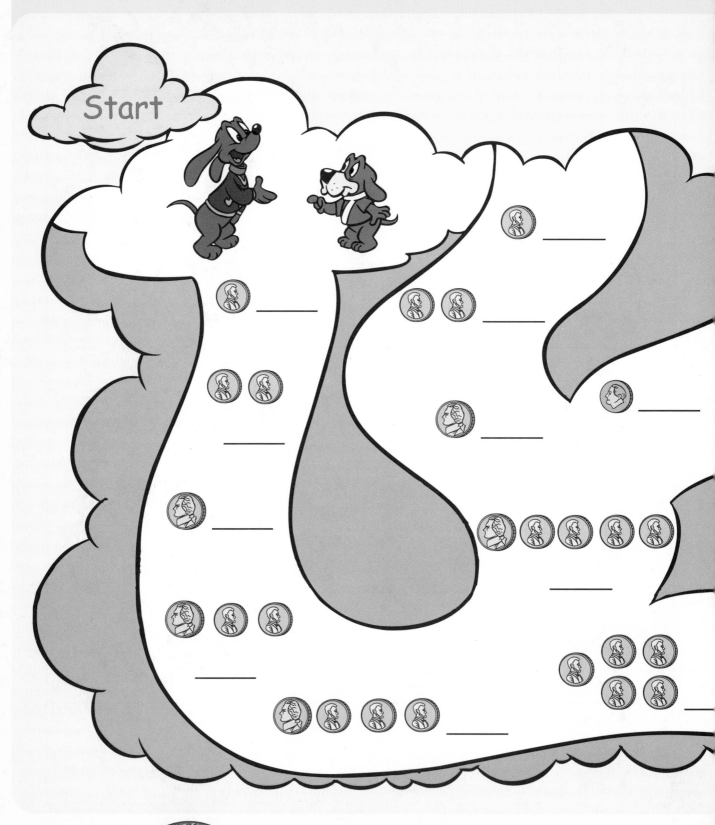

Write the amount near each coin or group of coins. Then draw a line along the correct path.

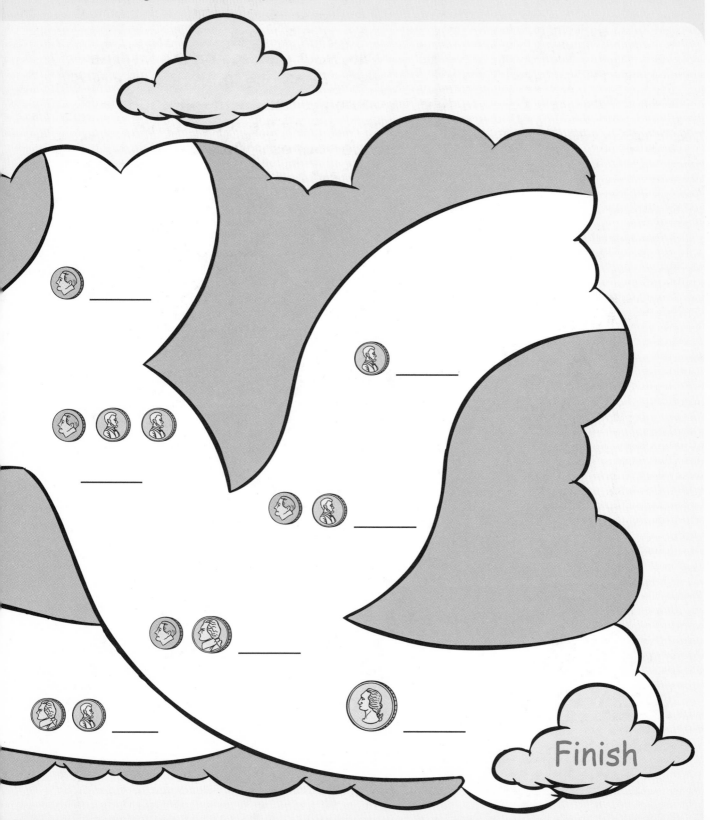

Finish

Great job! Put your money sticker on your Certificate of Completion and jump ahead!

Review (277)

Frankie's Facts

When you **estimate**, you make a rough **guess** about an amount or measurement.

Oops! I dropped my bag of jelly beans. How many jelly beans are in each pile? Wait! Don't count them yet! Estimate!

Write your guesses on the first line under each pile. Then go back and count the piles. Write the actual amounts on the second line. Were your estimates close?

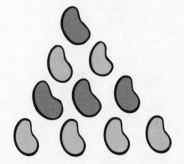

_____   _____   _____

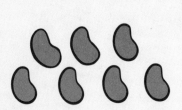
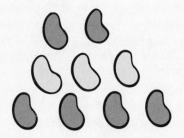
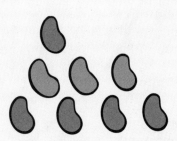

_____   _____   _____

Yum! Floyd and I are baking cupcakes.
Guess how many sprinkles are on each cupcake. Write the number on the first line. Then go back and count the sprinkles. Write the actual number on the second line. How many times did you estimate right?

Great! Put your coin sticker on your money sack and jump ahead to the next level.

Estimation (279)

Floyd and I have to figure out how many hot dogs to make for each class.

In each class, guess how many groups of five there are. Count the children and write the actual number on the line.

_____

_____

_____

_____

_____

_____

How many children are in your class?

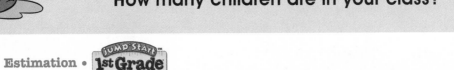

Now we need forks, spoons, and cups. Floyd has **14** children in his class, and I have **19**. Do we have enough?

First, estimate and write your guess on the first line. Then count and write the actual number on the second line. Cross out the groups of things that are not enough for each of our classes.

_____

_____

_____

We've just finished scooping tall ice-cream sundaes!
How many scoops high is each sundae?
Take a good guess and write it on the first line.
Then count them and write the answer on the second line. Color them your favorite colors!

It's cleanup time!

Look at all these bubbles. Estimate how many are in each bowl. Write your estimate on the first line. Then count the bubbles and write the actual amount on the second line.

You really cleaned up! Put your coin sticker on your money sack and jump ahead to the next level!

Estimation   283

Frankie's Facts

You can also estimate **length** (how long something is), **weight** (how heavy something is), or **temperature** (how hot something is).

We're getting close to the end of the school day, so it's time to celebrate with a cake. How big and how heavy do you think it is? **Circle the answers you think are correct.**

length	5 inches	24 inches	30 inches
weight	lighter than a bowling ball	the same weight as a bowling ball	heavier than a bowling ball

These are some of our favorite foods. Each thermometer shows how hot or cold each food is.

Draw a line from each thermometer to the food you think is about the same temperature.

Great guessing! Put your coin sticker on your money sack and jump ahead!

Floyd and I had a lot of fun. We hope you did, too! Now let's go on a treasure hunt!

coins in the treasure chest

10 50

noisemakers

10 4

bananas

8 12

Estimate each answer and then circle the correct one.

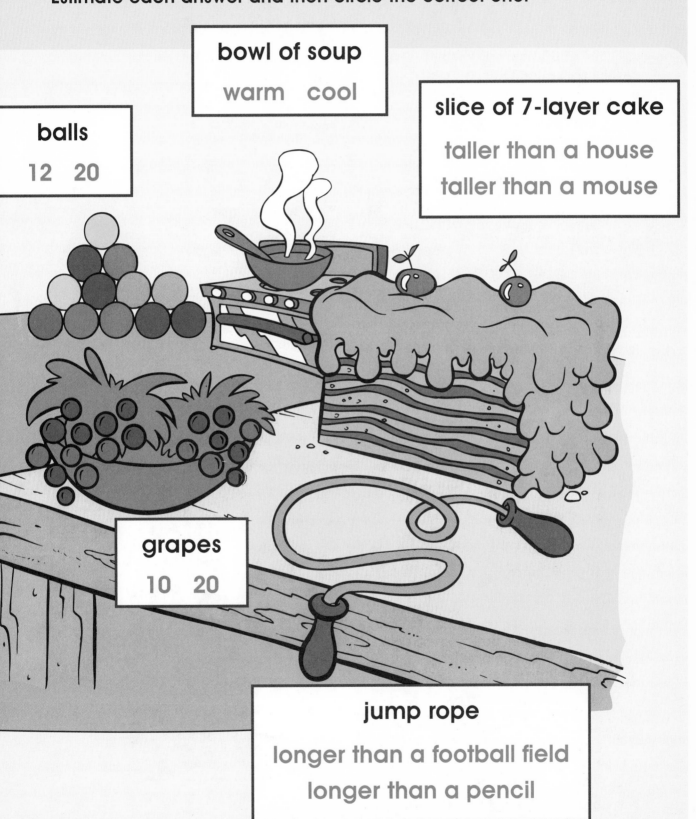

bowl of soup

warm   cool

slice of 7-layer cake

taller than a house

taller than a mouse

balls

12   20

grapes

10   20

jump rope

longer than a football field

longer than a pencil

You're the big winner! Put your plate sticker on your Certificate of Completion!

Review   287

Answer Key

PAGE 258   trace clock numbers

PAGE 259   connect 3 o'clock, 7 o'clock, 10 o'clock, 6 o'clock, 2 o'clock; color clocks

PAGE 260   draw hour hand at 9, 1, 11, 12, 4

PAGE 261   draw minute hand pointing to 12 on all, and hour hand pointing to 8, 10, 12, 1, 3

PAGE 262   write 9, 10, 11, 12, 1

PAGE 263   write 10/10, 11/11, 12/12; color music room door red, art room yellow, classroom green, lunchroom blue

PAGE 264   write 9:00, 10:30, 12:00, 1:30, 2:30

PAGE 265   draw hour hand/minute hand at 8/6, 11/6, 9/6, 12/6, 10/12, 1/12

PAGES 266–267   draw path line from 1:00 to 2:00 to 3:00 to 4:00 to 5:00 to 6:00 to 7:00 to 8:00 to 12:00

PAGE 268   trace numbers

PAGE 269   connect penny with apple, bread, banana; nickel with hot dog, jam, watermelon

PAGE 270   draw 5 pennies, 10 pennies; middle shelf; color 5¢ sign green; bottom shelf; color 10¢ sign blue

PAGE 271   draw 10 pennies, 1 dime, 1 nickel and 5 pennies

PAGE 272   connect to watermelon 10 pennies, 1 nickel and 5 pennies, 2 nickels, 1 dime

PAGE 273   draw 5 pennies, 10 pennies

PAGE 274   write 25¢, 10¢, 34¢, 35¢, 5¢

PAGE 275   write 31¢, 9¢, 8¢, 9¢, 35¢, 5¢

PAGES 276–277   write in the correct amounts; draw path line through these filled-in amounts; 1¢, 2¢, 5¢, 7¢, 8¢, 9¢, 10¢, 12¢, 15¢, 25¢

PAGE 278   answers will vary; write 6, 10, 4, 7, 9, 8

PAGE 279   answers will vary; write 7, 6, 8, 8, 4, 10; answers will vary

PAGE 280   write 5, 10, 15, 5, 10, 15

PAGE 281   answers will vary; write under Frankie 22, 17, 20; write under Floyd 15, 15, 13; cross out spoons under Frankie, cross out cups under Floyd

PAGE 282   answers will vary; write 12, 9, 15, 18; color scoops

PAGE 283   answers will vary; write 14, 6, 20, 11, 8, 15

PAGE 284   circle 5 inches, lighter than a bowling ball

PAGE 285   connect freezing/ice cream, cold/milk, hot/soup

PAGES 286–287   circle 50, 10, 8, warm, 12, taller than a mouse, 20, longer than a pencil

Hi, kids! It's Frankie here with a new spin on things. This globe I'm sitting on shows you what the earth is like. Where do you think it might take us? Come along and find out!

See these coin stickers? Every time you learn something new, you get one of these stickers to put in your money sack. When you finish a whole section, you'll get a big treasure sticker to put on the Certificate of Completion at the end of the book.

See this picture of me? When you see it in the book, it means I'm there to give you a little help. Just look for **Frankie's Facts**.

OK! Let's go for a spin.

Frankie's Facts

Plants, animals, and people are alive. They are **living things**.

The chalkboard, the desk, and the window are not alive. They are **non–living things**.

living   non–living

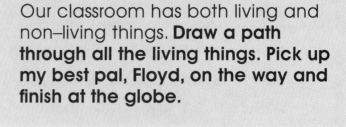

Our classroom has both living and non–living things. **Draw a path through all the living things. Pick up my best pal, Floyd, on the way and finish at the globe.**

Start

Finish

Our first adventure is to the rain forest! **Circle six living things.**
Cross out five things that are non–living.

Great! Put your coin sticker on your money sack and jump ahead!

Living Things 291

Spin the globe! Now we're in a hot grassland. This baboon is here to greet us. **Look at the arrows with matching colors. What things do you see that are the same? Write the words on the lines. Choose from the words in the box.**

| nose | eyes | ears | legs | mouth |

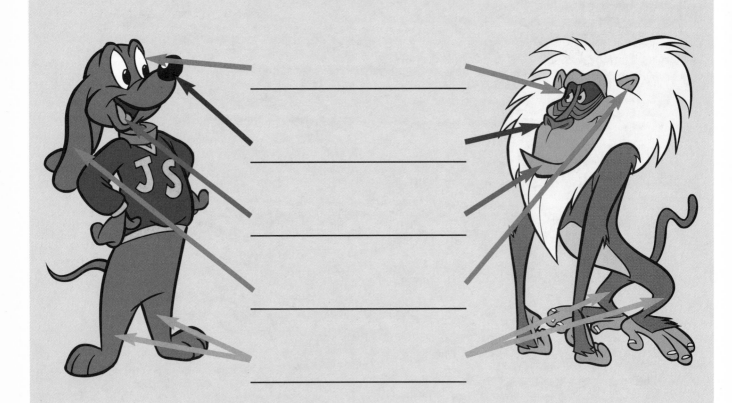

_____

_____

_____

_____

_____

Frankie's Facts

Some animals have **hair** or **fur** to cover them. Birds have **feathers**. Fish and snakes have **scales**.

All this globe–spinning is making me a little dizzy. Now I'm at the city wildlife park, a great place to see lots of animals. **Circle the animals with fur. Put an X on the animals with feathers. Underline the animals with scales.**

I'm supposed to set these three lost animals on the right paths. Can you help me? **Draw a line from each animal to the correct path. Choose a word from the box that tells how the animals are the same. Write it on the line under the path.**

| scales | fur | feathers |

  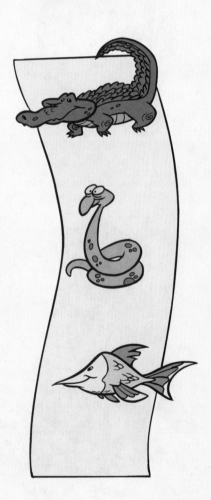

_____   _____   _____

Frankie's Facts

Plants can make their own food from **sunlight**, **water**, and **air**. Animals can't.

Which of these things is a plant? Which is an animal? **Color all the plants green. Color the animals any way you like.**

Excellent! Put your coin sticker on your money sack and jump ahead to the next level.

Animals, animals everywhere! **Find and circle all the animal names in the puzzle. Look at the pictures for clues.**

WORM

CRAB

OCTOPUS

```
O C T O P U S W E
A R E E N K M B L
S S N A I L Y O U
S W O R M C R A B
E S E A S T A R E
B U T T E R F L Y
```

SNAIL

SEA STAR

BUTTERFLY

What do these animals eat? **Read each sentence. Draw a line to match the animal to the correct plant. Then draw the matching plant in each animal picture.**

Giraffes eat leaves.

Bears eat berries.

Squirrels eat nuts.

Deer eat grass.

Can you think of another animal that eats plants? _____

Good job! Put your coin sticker on your money sack and jump ahead.

Living Things (297)

Before we go, I have another puzzle to figure out. Some of these animals are alike in certain ways. **Draw lines to match each pair of similar animals. Read each clue and match the animals it describes.**

CLUES

We are big and have lots of fur.

Our heads have hard, pointed parts called tusks.

We have scales and we slither.

We have fur and spots.

We have scales and live underwater.

We have feathers.

Fantastic! Put your parrot sticker on your Certificate of Completion. Now jump ahead!

Review 299

Do you like sunny or cloudy weather? How about rainy or snowy? **For each picture, write the word from the box that describes the kind of weather. Circle the weather you like best. Then color all the pictures.**

sunny   snowy   windy
rainy   cloudy

_____   _____

_____

_____   _____

Frankie's Facts

A small picture called a **symbol** can stand for a kind of weather.

sunny

rainy

Have you ever read the weather report in the newspaper? Maybe you can help me figure it out. **Look at the symbols in the middle of the page. Draw a line from each symbol to the kind of weather it stands for. Then color the pictures.**

Good work! Put your coin sticker on your money sack and jump ahead to the next level!

Weather 301

Frankie's Facts

There are four seasons every year. They are: **winter**, **spring**, **summer**, and **fall**.

Brrr! What season of the year do you think it is? **Look at the picture. Then read the sentences and fill in the blanks. Choose from the words in the box.**

cold	**snow**
winter	**sled**
ice	**snowman**

This season is _____.

The weather can get very _____.

When it does, the lake freezes into _____.

Sometimes _____ falls in flakes from the sky.

If there is enough of it, you can build a _____.

You can also ride down a hill on a _____.

The seasons sure change fast around here. It's spring already!
Color all the spring things in the picture. Then put an X on the one thing that does not belong in spring.

Now add your own spring thing to the middle of the picture.

Summertime! Look at all these shells. Some have summer words on them, and some have winter words. **Read the word on each shell. Color all the summer shells yellow. Color the winter shells blue.**

ice

baseball

sunny

sled

snow

swim

beach

shorts

hot

cold

In many places in the fall, the leaves turn beautiful colors and then fall from the trees. **Make your own colorful fall picture. Match the number on each leaf to a color in the box. Color in the leaves!**

1 = red   2 = orange   3 = yellow   4 = brown

You're bright! Put your coin sticker on your money sack and jump ahead!

As Floyd and I hop around the globe, we must be ready for all kinds of weather. Help us decide what to wear. **Draw a line from each symbol to the right clothes for that kind of weather. Then draw a picture of yourself wearing clothes during your favorite season.**

I can find something to do in any weather! What kind of weather is in each of these pictures? **Unscramble the words and write them on the lines. Choose from the words in the box.**

| rainy | snowy | windy | sunny |

yunns

_____

inary

_____

yowns

_____

dniwy

_____

Excellent! Put your coin sticker on your money sack and jump ahead!

Weather 307

What a fun trip around the globe! Now help us do these puzzles.

Look at each picture. Then look at the word box and write the word that tells the season.

On the next line, write the word that tells the weather.

Next number the seasons in order from 1 to 4 beginning with winter.

Now circle the season and weather words in the word find.

_____

_____

1 _____

_____

_____

_____

_____

_____

WORD BOX

spring	fall	winter	summer
sunny	rainy	windy	snowy

WORD FIND

```
S U M W F A L L
N N W I N T E R
O T S N E T R A
W I R D T W I I
Y S I Y N I A N
S U M M E R R Y
W N S P R I N G
A N S U N N Y Y
```

Good job! Put your snowflake sticker on your Certificate of Completion and jump ahead.

Review (309)

Frankie's Facts

The enviroment is different everywhere. Some places on earth are very cold all the time. Some are very hot.

Floyd and I are looking at our globe again. We're wondering where on earth it's hottest and where it's coldest. **The number under each line below stands for a letter in the alphabet. Look at the letter key to match numbers to letters. Write each letter on the line and read the answers.**

1 = A	5 = E	9 = I	13 = M	17 = Q	21 = U	25 = Y
2 = B	6 = F	10 = J	14 = N	18 = R	22 = V	26 = Z
3 = C	7 = G	11 = K	15 = O	19 = S	23 = W	
4 = D	8 = H	12 = L	16 = P	20 = T	24 = X	

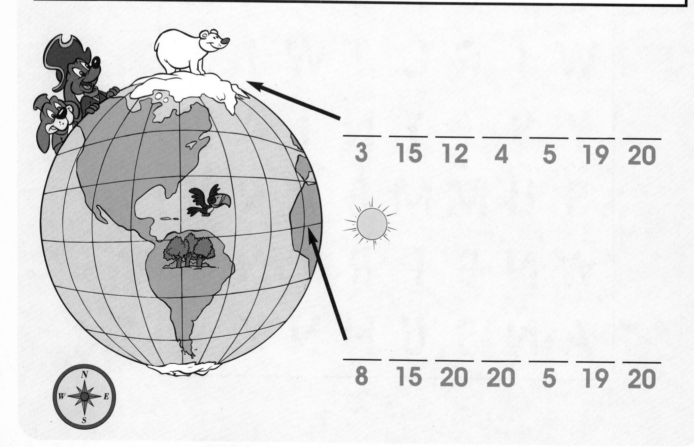

___ ___ ___ ___ ___ ___ ___
3 15 12 4 5 19 20

___ ___ ___ ___ ___ ___ ___
8 15 20 20 5 19 20

The first postcard shows a hot place and the second shows a cold place. **In each picture there are two things that don't belong. Put an X on them.**

You did it! Put your coin sticker on your money sack and jump ahead!

Environment 311

Frankie's Facts

Different places have different **environments**. Some places in the world have lots of trees and plants. Some places are very dry and some are very wet.

It's fall now! Come take a walk in the woods with us. **For each woodsy animal or plant listed below, find something in the picture that begins with the same letter. Write it on the line. Look in the word box for help.**

bush	**f**ern	**r**abbit
squirrel	**m**ouse	

berries _____   **m**ushroom _____

raccoon _____   **f**ox _____

spider _____